Peter

THE WATERMEADOW
MYSTERY

THE SECRET TREASURE AT
HAWTON

AUSTIN MACAULEY PUBLISHERS™

LONDON · CAMBRIDGE · NEW YORK · SHARJAH

A CIP catalogue record for this title is available from the British Library.

ISBN 9781528910590 (Paperback)
ISBN 9781528910606 (E-Book)

www.austinmacauley.com

First Published (2018)
Austin Macauley Publishers Ltd™
25 Canada Square
Canary Wharf
London
E14 5LQ

Acknowledgements

This book would not have been written but for the enactment of a play performed on the 1st July, 2017, in which the principal characters were Daniel and Fiona Hubery, Helen Tyrer, Janet O'Donoghue, James Fry, Steve Cawte, Steve Watson, Gilles and Noella Coulombeau. Their acting was so convincing that all present on the occasion were so caught up in the plot that even the most sceptical were taken in. So I thank all of them for germinating the people who are the centrepiece of this book.

Author's Note

Although many of the places mentioned in this book are genuine, the characters portrayed are either entirely fictitious or if genuine, have attributes or statements of language that are fictitious. But it is also true that King James, in travelling south from Edinburgh to London in 1603, spent a considerable time in the East Midlands, was short of ready cash, and responded by creating new knights of the realm in exchange for money and valuable goods. How much of these remained in the East Midlands is not known. As for Watermeadow, although the Estate to the south of Hawton described in the book does not exist, King James was sufficiently stimulated by the sight of the marshes in Hawton to make the draining of the watermeadow just north of Westminster a priority of his reign, and so created a royal park, the St James's Park of today. And for those interested in cricket and the expectations of Arthur Mansfield, Don Bradman scored 7 runs for Australia in the first innings of the Third Test at Old Trafford in July 1948, and 30 not out in the second. The match was drawn.

Table of Contents

Chapter 1
Frothy Looks Forward to the Party

Lord Frothy Watermeadow was feeling pleased with life, with his surroundings, with his friends and family, but, most of all, with himself. For the first time in what he considered an age, things were looking up. The war was over, times were hardly good but people were pretty civilised in their dealings with each other, and his gout was now hardly troubling him at all. And, even though the government had no money, they were going to set up a National Health Service next Monday, where all treatment would be given 'free at the point of need'. Now that was a revolution in the making – as long as they weren't expecting him to pay for it.

He reflected on all these pleasant prospects as he was returning from the Watermeadow Golf Course, where had actually won a tournament – well, more like an elderly pitch and putt contest – but he had been working on his short game and for once, his clubs had been listening to him.

The weather was also good for a party. It had been a fairly cool summer since the hot days at the end of May, but in July it was better to have an event like this when it was not too hot yet still dry, so there would be no mud on the carpets. He passed Hawton Church, noting the shrapnel damage to the tower wall from a stray bomb that had landed on the road in 1942 and comparing it with the musket ball damage to the west door, a few feet away, dating from the Civil War three centuries earlier. Oh, how little mankind had changed!

There had been some argument in the church about the repairs. Some had insisted the bells, which were getting pretty decrepit since they were put up in the 15th century, would fall down if nothing was done to repair the tower. Fortunately, an anonymous donor had stumped up all the money needed for the restoration of what was, after all, a pretty impressive tower for such a small village.

But what really cheered Frothy was the thought of his grand party this evening on a date he was sure everyone at Watermeadow would remember, at least for a few weeks, and if all went well, possible for years to come. He repeated to himself '3, 7, 4, 8'; the 3rd July, 1948. There was a symmetry about these numbers that appealed, the 4 and 8 indicating the steady advance on the 3 and 7.

Of course there was a reason for the party. The vicar of Hawton, the Reverend David Milliner, was retiring, and as he was such a popular fellow, it was only right that he should have a proper send off. But his retirement was only an excuse for Frothy's party. This would be the occasion to tell the world that the Watermeadow Estate would, for the first time in 200 years, be in credit with the world. This was not a bad message to tell all his guests at a time of national debt – Watermeadow would light the way forward.

As he walked up the drive, Frothy mused about the history of the estate. It was 1655, he recalled, that his ancestor, Colonel Philip Endewler, bought the southern Newark marshes, following his reward for backing the winner, Oliver Cromwell, in the Civil War. After the successful drainage of the marshes, Watermeadow House was built on the higher land and opened to great pomp and acclaim, with all the townspeople of Hawton in attendance 12 years later. The golden years of Watermeadow followed, with visitors from across the country, including the Prince Regent in 1816 after the battle of Waterloo, where the little woodland by the edge of the marsh where he had tea with Maria, his paramour, is still called Prinny's Folly.

But Frothy's great-grandfather, Lord Samuel Watermeadow, nicknamed Squashy after his habit of always walking around the estate, and often the house, in Wellington boots, started the decline, by his fascination for gambling.

What a legacy, Frothy still fumed whenever he thought about it, *£500,000 of assets converted to £350,000 of squalid debts in less than 15 years, by always guessing wrong.* So every subsequent Watermeadow heir had been forced to chisel away at reducing the debt, or Squashy's Mess as it was called, not really with any great success, so that when Frothy inherited the Watermeadow Estate in 1925, over £200,000 was still owing to creditors.

'But now all that will be a thing of the past,' said Frothy to himself, as he saw Steve the gardener, who dutifully touched his cap and lowered his head as Frothy passed by. The announcement of the recent acquisition of the six acres to the east of the church, or the Hawton Six as they were commonly called, was already known to many people. What was not known, and would be announced by Frothy at the party, was that gold had been found in the Hawton Six just by the Watermeadow boundary. Dr Rock Solid, a geologist, who had known Frothy for years, had discovered the gold, not far beneath the surface, and now that the land was part of the Watermeadow Estate, it would be added to their assets. Quite a few of the Watermeadow creditors would be at the party, and Frothy could not wait to tell them that before long, he would be able now to lend – and never borrow – again.

Chapter 2
Rock Glitters

Rock Solid was discomfited and tense, but also a little excited, as he walked about the carefully constructed gardens of Watermeadow House. He had never been a happy man, but for the first time in his life, he felt that happiness might be, if not just around the corner, at least at a bend in the distance. Fate had been stacked against him for years but might shortly be coming over to his side. He had known the Watermeadow family for years – but they had used him, and he was annoyed that he had only just realised this. He had left school early because Lord Frothy had offered him an attractive post as a geologist. Now geology was a proper 'ology' and to the young Rock was a path to a glittering career as a scientist. And so it seemed at first. He dabbled away at soil and rock analysis in the Watermeadow Estate and was able to get a place at the University of Rockingham just before the war started, where he completed his PhD in record time in 1940.

They had queried his name for his PhD. But he never regretted changing his name by deed poll from the prissy one attached to him when he was born, Roy Solliss, to the macho Rock Solid. 'Poor little boy, I think he wants a bit of solace,' they used to tease him at school. It all stopped when he became Rock Solid. This was a good way to earn respect.

He joined up and served in North Africa at a time when military geology was just becoming important. He saw little front-line action as his skills were needed, and greatly appreciated, in planning the sites of airfields in Libya and getting water supplies in the desert. He then moved with the advancing Eighth Army to Italy, but was held up for months at Monte Cassino in the advance on Rome, and this was where his geological skills were of little value.

He ruminated about this time as he strolled round the garden, knowing that some of his war-time skills might be needed in the months ahead. People always assumed that even though war was awful, it must always be exciting, but the Battle of Monte Cassino was anything but exciting, sitting for months waiting for bombers to decimate the German defenders on the hill above. Despite destroying every building they could see, the resistance never faltered, and they were stuck for months.

But there were amusing moments. Rock remembered one young man, Gunner Milligan was his name, who kept them in stitches with his zany observations on military life. 'Looks like a messenger from the front,' he once said when he saw a weary adjutant coming down the track; 'looks like a messenger from the back too,' he added as the figure passed them on his way down to headquarters. Rock chuckled again as he thought about these times and sang under his breath,

'We're the D-Day Dodgers out in Italy
Always on the vino, always on the spree
Eighth Army scroungers and their tanks
We live in Rome – among the Yanks,
We are the D-Day Dodgers,
Over here in Italy.'

But many of them would have preferred being on the D-Day landings than sitting like oversized brown grubs on an exposed and windy hillside, waiting and waiting for something – anything – to happen.

When the war ended it was a bit of an anticlimax. Nobody seemed to want geologists in peacetime, and Frothy had taken him back to Watermeadow. But he was paid a ludicrously small salary, only £100 a year more than he had before he went to university, so he hardly felt valued.

But then Frothy came to him one day with a suggestion that stirred some enthusiasm. 'Rock,' Frothy had said, 'I have a hunch there's gold in the Watermeadow Estate. There have been stories about gold around here ever since Hawton (or Holtone as it was called then) was first described in the Domesday Book. Carried down by the river, they said, some grains found in the foundations when the church was built in 1350 but nothing since. Now if anyone can find this gold, it's my man, Rock Solid. Are you game?'

Rock was only half enticed. Being generally pessimistic by nature – his mother said he always found trouble hidden behind every treasure – he could easily dismiss this suggestion as the fancy of an elderly man who had little to excite him. But, even if he was only half right, the search for gold was something new and of much greater interest than his usual job of measuring the height of the water table and assessing the risk of flooding. In any case, there was little choice. Nothing else was available, so Rock accepted the offer, but with a hefty dose of scepticism. It seemed inconceivable that gold would be found at Watermeadow. There was no quartz for miles, and no exposed rocks, and all the old gold mines were in Wales or Scotland. But Frothy was right in thinking there had been much talk about gold in the marshes ever since mediaeval times, and it would be surprising if it was total fiction.

So Rock diligently set to work at the edge of the Watermeadow Estate, at a place where Frothy was insistent gold had been found in the past. Chris Challis, the head gardener and landscape architect, was very choosy about the areas he would allow to be prospected, so Rock was forced to go to areas where he would never have thought could ever contain gold, or indeed silver or lead.

But shortly afterwards, and very surprisingly, within six months of prospecting and analysing, he found pockets of black sand – always a good indicator that gold might be around – only 20 feet below the surface, extending outwards to the east, just beyond the boundary of the Watermeadow Estate.

So Rock made a tunnel to explore further, shored it up with timbers and a roof of old planks, and continued to analyse the soil and their deposits as he moved eastward. And then, quite unexpectedly, one late afternoon, as he shone his torch into the newly excavated area, the light reflected straight back. Two tiny gold grains had been exposed. Rock was amazed. He carefully removed the balls of rock and earth containing the grains and took them back to his lab (really a glorified tent with a sink and tap inside) to clean them. Finally, he came to Frothy with his news.

Frothy, as usual, greeted him exuberantly. 'Always nice to see you, Rock, any news to report? You seem pretty pleased with yourself. You know, Cheshire cat smile and all that.'

Rock said nothing, but merely took out his small bag of chamois leather, opened it, and let two small shining heavy flakes – not quite nuggets – of gold drop onto the table in front of Frothy.

Even Frothy was speechless for a moment. 'I've weighed them,' said Rock, 'one and a half ounces, worth £63 at today's prices.' So, for the first time in their lives, Frothy and Rock had something really in common; the thought that they would no longer have to worry about debt. The bright sky of financial solvency for both of them beckoned in the distance. But would it ever be overhead?

Chapter 3
1603 – An Interrupted Journey

'Ding, deng, ding dong,' rang the bells, not entirely tunefully, from Hawton Church across the fields and marshes. If we could peep through the louvres, we would see Albert Sergeant, William Mitchell, Thomas Exton and Henry Hooton hard at work ringing Plain Bob Minimus on the four bells in the tower. But they were all puzzled.

'Can't think for the life of me why the Rector 'ad to ask us to ring the bells this morning,' complained Albert. 'What it bein' a Tuesday and no service an' all.'

'Keep yer 'and on the sally and stop grumblin',' Thomas responded, 'what 'as to be done 'as to be done.'

'And we are getting a ha'penny each for our troubles,' added William, 'can't be all bad.'

With Plain Bob Minimus finished, the four made their way gingerly down the steps to the floor of the church below. It was a warm April day, and they were sweating underneath their thick woollen smocks after the energetic ringing in the enclosed bell tower.

As they stepped out into the open sunshine, they heard the sound of horses in the distance. 'Must be a hunt on today,' muttered Henry. 'Lot of riders there, I bet.' He was right. The noise of galloping hooves scattered the starlings from the trees and a few moments later the bell-ringers, now joined by the Rector Francis Clarke, were surrounded by horsemen in plumed helmets, followed shortly by a carriage where a small man was seated, elegantly dressed and half hidden in folds of silken finery.

'Make way for the king!' shouted the leader of the group, seated on a fine black stallion. This was unnecessary as the king showed no sign of moving.

'Didn't know we 'ad a king', muttered Albert. 'Last time I 'eard we 'ad a queen – what's 'appened to 'er?' An explanation was necessary, and it soon followed.

'This is a royal journey,' said the black stallion rider. 'King James of Scotland is now also King James of England, so attend now – bow your heads before your new sovereign.'

The four men shuffled forward in embarrassment and sheepishly lifted their caps, lowering their heads just enough to pay homage without wanting to commit themselves to something that might turn out to be a sham. Francis followed behind but came to the front as they approached the carriage, took off his square Canterbury cap and bowed.

'Greetings from our village, your Royal Highness, I trust the sound of the bells helped you to find us.'

The man in the carriage looked at them quizzically. He did not really look like a king, but you could never tell nowadays who was who.

'Aye, it did, thanks,' he answered, now leaning forward. 'Whaur's this village then, and whaur ar ye people frae?' he asked, looking at them closely. With some help in translation from his guards, most of whom seemed to be from Scotland, it seemed as though the king wanted to know full details about the village where he had just appeared out of the blue.

Francis cleared his throat.

'This is the village of Hawton, sire (he was not sure if "sire" was right at the second time of asking, but nobody interrupted). It is close to the town of Newark but we are proud to be our own village, with our farms, our shop, our village hall, and, of course, our magnificent church, which you can see just behind us.'

King James had had enough.

'Haud yer wheesht,' he interrupted. 'We'll stay here.'

The royal party was obviously listening closely to every word from the king, as they immediately dismounted and asked where they might stay. It looked as though the king had taken a shine to Hawton and would be around for some time.

Chapter 4
Lady Aqua Gets Ready

Lady Aqua was restless. There was so much to do today, and she did not know where to start. After walking around aimlessly for a few minutes, she suddenly realised, 'When in doubt, wash your hair.' This had served her well for 30 years, and it was going to work again now. And it did.

That lovely feeling of serenity, a mixture of contentment, calm and inner confidence, had come over her as she dried her hair in front of the large mirror by the four-poster bed in the main Watermeadow bedroom. She was Sarah again for a moment, Sarah being a massively self-confident girl she knew at school, and whom she had always admired for her hair. But then the feeling disappeared, pretty quickly, as she started thinking about the day ahead – why did thinking always have to get in the way? There was so much to do before the party. She folded a blank piece of paper, lengthways, and started on her list. The weather was fine and warm, so there was no need to light any fires, and Maggie, her reliable factotum, would ensure that all the reception rooms were in good order.

Her main concern was the kitchen. Catering for at least 40, and possibly 60, people was always difficult when you did not know how many people are going to come and what they would and would not eat. Aqua could not understand why everybody was not an omnivore. Primitive man was not fussy about his food, so why had everybody started to get finicky in recent years, and this has happened in spite of rationing and the war. In the end, she decided the people with food fads must just be using a way of making themselves remembered.

If you told your host you would only eat beef, cabbage and duchess potatoes, you could hardly be forgotten in a crowd.

So when she started writing her list, everything possible had to be included. Meat (mainly lamb and beef), fish (fresh trout from the river), potatoes (the early ones were marvellous at this time of year), the second crop of peas, the early cabbages, and, of course, the desserts – blancmange (although she could not understand how anyone could eat something so slimy), raspberries and strawberries from the Watermeadow kitchen garden, greengage tart, lemon meringue pie, summer puddings – yes, just thinking about them stimulated and cheered her despite the worries of the day to come. Fred Spicer would be arriving at 10 o'clock in his little van and she had made sure almost everything needed would be there, fresh as fresh could be. And, as for rationing, she and Fred had a special arrangement that avoided all that nonsense. Grand rural houses always had access to the granaries of plenty – did people really want everything to rot in the fields?

But as she finished her list, the next set of thoughts were forced into her mind. These were both enticing and threatening. Had Frothy really found the answer to all his debts? Was there gold on the Watermeadow Estate? Could Rock Solid be trusted? There were too many imponderables. It would be so much better if all these doubts could be set aside and she could relax in certainty.

Every time she had seen Rock, she was troubled. He was furtive but also glib, smiling insincerely as he told her about his excavations in the estate. 'I can assure you, Lady Aqua (he always exaggerated the word "Lady" as though it could be equally a term of derision as respect), 'you will **not** be disappointed. I cannot say too much but it is all going really well.' The trouble was that Frothy failed to pick up the signs. He was far too trusting and regarded Rock like a faithful retainer, who would always be loyal and consistent, as Frothy had done so much for him.

But this was not the case at all. Aqua had seen Rock looking at Frothy when he was expounding at length (usually about matters that could be expressed much more economically), and there was clear derision on his face. No, Rock was not a man to be trusted.

If only Rock was no longer in the Watermeadow Estate and could be taken out of the gold equation. He was a tiresome interloper and, without him, everything would be so much simpler.

Chapter 5
King James Digs in His Heels

It was now 15th April, in the year of our Lord 1603. King James and his party were still in Hawton, and showing no desire to leave. The king had invited himself to stay with Gascon Cordonnier, a French woollen merchant who lived to the east of Hawton Church. James rightly worked out that Gascon was a Catholic, and as he felt so much more comfortable in the company of those of his own religion than others, he knew he would be happier there. Gascon and his wife, Noeleen, were only too pleased to have a real king staying with them, but immediately retired to the garret in the corner of the house when the king arrived as they did not want to be in his way. But James was not going to exclude them, and on the evening before, he had asked them to talk about Hawton and life in the village.

'The kirk, a' mean the church, dae ye ken these "Anglicans" there?' James knew he would have to come to terms with the many people in his expanded kingdom now he was the king of all the Scots and all the English, but he was very ignorant of the Protestant Church of England.

'Il n'ya pas a problem,' said Gascon, is his broken English, 'zey come and go into the church, and smile when zey see me, but zey are no bother – and ils chant – they sing – very nicely on the Sunday mornings. We open the windows to hear them.'

'Aye', said James, 'but do they ask ye to pray wi' em?'

'Non,' said Gascon clearly, 'zey do not.'

'Guid,' said James quietly and sat back in his chair. If he was able to keep the differences away from these two religions, he would have a better chance of bringing them together. But, despite this reassurance, he still felt a little uncomfortable in the morning looking out of his window at the great, but mildly menacing, frame of Hawton Church and its impressive curvilinear east window.

Better than most kirks in Edinburgh, he thought, *and this is only a village. Is the rest of England like this as well?*

But this did not put off James from enjoying the spring weather in this interlude of time on his way down from Edinburgh to London. It was quickly made clear to the villagers that the king could not arrive in London until after the funeral of Queen Elizabeth on 28th April. It would not look good for the new king to appear hasty. A slow and magisterial arrival would impress the citizens of this country so much more.

But the Scottish soldiers guessed that James would leave Hawton within a day or two and were surprised by his relaxed attitude towards the village. At the very least, they expected him to spend time in Stamford or Cambridge rather than this out of the way place in the north of Nottinghamshire. But they were unaware of an important item that was missing in King James's train – money. Scotland was not a rich country and could not compete with the munificence of the average English town, never mind the villages. But it must never be known that James was a penurious king. He realised the more generous he could be, the more popular he would become. But while he was in the early process of generating wealth, he felt much more at home in Hawton than Oxford, Cambridge and all these other towns of conspicuous wealth, who seemed to whisper 'pauper, pauper' incessantly as he passed by their grand exteriors.

So he hit on an idea to solve his financial problems, but he could only discuss this with his tiny group of financial advisers. Most people in Scotland did not know how poor he was. Only his comptroller, Sir David Murray of Gospertie, understood the parlous state of the royal purse. James used to receive a pension of £4000 annually from Elizabeth, but she had suddenly stopped this for no reason at a time when James was beginning to spend more in anticipation of moving south. Sir David was with him in Hawton, and, as the money dribbled away on the journey south, eventually had to tell him baldly, 'Ye're knacker'd, Jamie, skint, absolutely skint.'

No one else could talk like that to King James. But the king certainly was skint. But then Sir David had an idea, but like all good ideas in the royal court, it could not be implemented unless the king himself believed it was his idea. Queen Elizabeth had become less generous towards her people in her later years and had not created any knights for over 10 years. Many of the earlier ones had let her down, and she was compelled to have them beheaded, and so it seemed wasteful to create too many new ones.

But Sir David realised that James was generous with knighthoods, as indeed he had been in his own case. When James was suddenly short of £250 ten years earlier, David had lent him the money, but when he feared he would never be repaid, James had knighted him, and nothing more was said. So, remembering this only too well, he suggested to James that if the message was spread around the rich counties of England that many people who felt worthy of being ennobled could indeed be knighted by their new king – for a suitable emolument – this might be a solution to the financial crisis.

James quickly agreed that this was a good idea and that, in any case, he had been thinking about this possibility for some time. So he called Rory Stewart, his most trusted messenger, to ride to Belvoir Castle, not far south of Hawton, to let the Duke of Rutland know that King James was so impressed with the people on his journey south that he was 'minded to add to the nobility of the East of England'. But this would come at a price, and 'money and chattels of all kinds to the sum of at least £500 for each honour' would need to be given to the king's treasury before any of these generous acts could be made.

But King James and the rest of his entourage could do nothing until Rory had returned from Belvoir Castle, and both

Sir David and his sovereign realised that negotiations would not be easy. So all were told that the stay in Hawton would be a little longer than all had thought, and the travelling Scots would have to bide their time.

But, whatever else happened, James did not want to return to Newark. He had no love for the town. He had only learnt about it as a child and that made him shudder. 'This was where King John died, laddie,' he was told. 'In a stinking garret, surrounded by enemies. Don't allow yersel' to be put in that position.' Of course, that was nearly 400 years ago, but the castle where John died seemed as forbidding as ever when he passed through Newark a few days ago.

And, of course, there was the cutpurse episode on the road just south of Newark. It was getting late when a crowd suddenly surrounded his coach and produced a miserable-looking man, with only one eye and wearing rags that hardly seemed attached to his body, they were so tattered and torn.

'What's up?' James asked.

'He's a thieving magpie, that's what. A cutpurse and pickpocket, pinches anything 'e can lay 'is 'ands on. What are you going to do with him?'

James really had no idea, but when a shout rang out, 'Hang him, hang him!' repeated in unison by the mob that had gathered round his coach, he had an easy solution. And, for the first time in England, the excitement, and the potential, of becoming king of both England and Scotland hit him. Here he was, with the ability to command life or death, and nobody, simply nobody, could contradict him. So the right response in this situation was an easy one. Nobody could harm him or his kingdom when no longer alive. So he agreed with the mob, and so by royal prerogative, the poor miscreant, screaming his innocence on the way, was taken to the field by the road and hanged from a hastily erected gallows.

The miserable fellow had not been charged or tried in court, and James was advised by David, his universal adviser, that to hang him without a trial was an error as this infringed the laws of Magna Carta. But James, who never liked being criticised, quoted pompously from his recently published book, *"True Law of Free Monarchies"* in which he explicitly stated that a king was subservient only to God, not to the laws of man. It was God who would judge him and 'stirre up such scourges as pleaseth Him' after James died, not before.

But despite mounting a robust defence, James was troubled that he had indeed made an error. 'A royal head must be worthy of the Crown' was a maxim that had been instilled into him as a child, and, at least on this occasion, his head may not have fitted satisfactorily. He had taken the easy way out.

But whatever the case, Newark was going to be out of bounds for his men. Hawton was a safe country village, and he felt very content to stay in the comfort of its unmarked boundaries, close to the church, where he could not feel more secure.

Chapter 6
Lady Delta Is Besotted

Lady Delta's head was buzzing. So much was going on inside it – she feared it would explode and she would have some sort of fit. The last month had been the most exciting in her life, and she wanted it to continue like this, even though there were risks around every corner.

It had all started when she was walking in the garden one afternoon. She was checking whether the first raspberries were ripe for the first pavlova of the season. She was not a great cook, but she loved pavlova and had mastered the not particularly difficult task of getting the meringue cooked for exactly the right time, so it was crisp and crunchy on the surface but soft and creamy inside. And raspberries and cream rounded it off perfectly.

She approached the raspberry canes in their little enclosure. Yes, the raspberries were just beginning to show their enticing bubbles of red, but only a few were ready to pick. She was concentrating hard to find the ones she could choose for the pavlova. Suddenly, a hand appeared from behind her and picked a raspberry just out of her reach.

'Sorry to bother you, Lady Delta.' She turned around in alarm, lost her footing and fell into the arms of Steve Pitchfork, the under-gardener. The next few seconds would stay with her as long as she lived. The feel of his powerful muscles, the musty smell of his gardening jacket and the warmth of his body combined to raise her to a peak of ecstasy that far exceeded the time she had won the Watermeadow Junior Dancing Competition at the age of eight (and then on reflection she felt the judges were probably biased). She had seen Steve from a distance before but never even thought about him. Now she could not stop thinking about him all the time.

'Oh, oh, oh!' said Delta, not the most informative of her utterances, but she was now in a different world where speech no longer mattered.

Steve was more coherent. 'I do 'ope I 'aven't upset you, Lady Delta, but I could see what you wanted and couldn't quite reach it.'

Lady Delta was forced to come to her senses. Yes, she now knew exactly what she wanted, and it was far from being out of reach. She was not going to leave the arms of Steve Pitchfork until he kissed her. Each time he tried to prop her up, she sunk into his arms again, opening her eyes large in invitation, and eventually, he got the message. She tingled all over. And as she walked back to Watermeadow House, she vowed she was not going to let him go.

Chapter 7
The Rector Receives a Visit

It was Thursday, 19th April, 1603, a useful non-event day in the church calendar, so Francis Clarke, the rector of Hawton Church, was relaxing. He was content. The last 14 years, since he became rector, had all been positive, and he could not have been happier. And to cap it all, that hearty lunch of bread, cheese and soup prepared so excellently by his good wife, Matilda, was allowing him this afternoon to slowly sink into a contented reverie.

He ruminated while he dozed. King James and his men were still in Hawton but generally were behaving well. True, there were a few squabbles with some of the more hot-headed villagers, and young Harry Harmington was at home nursing a broken elbow after an unwise argument, but it could have been so much worse. It had been a great help that these Scots had brought with them a new game. Francis was not quite sure what the idea behind it was, and it had an odd name. It sounded like "gofe" or was it "goff"; these Scots were so difficult to understand. King James had been fascinated by it and was determined to bring it to England, but he said this would be difficult as he needed wooden clubs and lots of flat grass to play it. What was even stranger was the main purpose of the game, to put a round ball into a hole. Well, odder things had happened in life, but how on earth could this be thought of as a game? He hoped it would not be followed by a suggestion that tossing balls of wool into the font at All Saints Church would liven up services; he would never allow this to happen. God forbid, indeed.

But he had to admit the game had been a boon to Hawton. The soldiers had all been tutored in the game and had made clubs out of the straight branches of the alder trees growing by the River Devon. They brought sheep onto the little patch of grass to the north of the church, and within a day or so, the grass was short enough to play the game. A series of holes was made with the edge of a ploughshare and a small cannonball was soon scooting across the green with shouts of 'On yer way, laddie!' from the Scottish soldiers. Before long, the Hawton villagers had learnt how to play as well. David Ditton, the parish clerk, was adept at picking up the rules and was soon in earnest competition with the best of the soldiers, and had prepared an elaborate score-slate to record the results.

Yes, there was no doubt that a good game was an antidote to war. He hoped that the king would be successful in bringing this goff game to England. There might even be friendly events with Protestants playing against Catholics. Perhaps not, it was just a little too much to expect at present, with feelings running so high.

A knock at the door disturbed this pleasant line of cooperative thought. Matilda opened it and Henry Webster, alderman of Newark, walked in confidently. John recognised the footsteps without looking up – nobody else clumped into his house quite like Henry Webster.

'I need a word with you, Francis, as I am quite discomfited.' Henry always came to the point immediately. There was too much of importance in his life for pleasantries. Matilda departed, realising her presence would be undesired. In any case, she could hear the mews of Plain Bob, the black cat who had been adopted by the bell-ringers in the tower as their mascot, and he was due his daily ration of milk. 'Come along, Peebee,' she said, stroking his sleek head, 'this will be an appetiser for the rat-hunting of the day.'

The two men faced each other warily in the drawing room. 'I am pleased to see you, Alderman Webster, and am always at your service.' (Francis had learnt to call Henry "Alderman" very early on; it was a title of which he was very proud. There was even talk about creating an Alderman's Walk in the town.)

'It has come to my notice, and indeed almost everybody else in the town of Newark, that our future king is staying in the village of Hawton. What do you mean by this?'

'I mean nothing, Alderman. King James arrived, quite unexpectedly, and decided he would stay, together with all his men. I had nothing to do with it.'

'Humph,' replied Henry. 'I find this very hard to believe. Do you not realise that it is perceived as an insult in the town that you did not choose to advise him that Newark was the appropriate place for him to stay, rather than this, dare I say, insignificant village on the road to Cotham and the south.'

'I do not choose to argue with King James, Alderman, and neither, I feel, should you. He seems to like it here; he has business to attend to that he does not wish to discuss with me, and I thought it politick to leave him to order his own affairs.'

'Inactivity is shameful when it is right to move. I suggest you let King James know that we expect him to travel to Newark to see the comfort and hospitality of the town – and then he can choose where to stay. I know what his decision would be.'

'I would be happy to do this, Alderman, but is Newark ready to see King James?'

'Of course, it is. I know that the burghers of Newark are all yearning to look after our future sovereign. And their terms are very modest.'

'Their terms might not meet with the approval of King James.'

'What are you saying, man? Of course, they will.'

'I need to tell you something, Alderman. King James has no money. We in Hawton are not receiving any payment for our hospitality.'

'What, nothing at all?'

'No, nothing. He says he will pay us – in time – but we do not have any hopes of receiving anything. He has said something about making Hawton a Royal Village, but we do not expect this to happen.'

'I certainly hope not,' expostulated Henry, getting to his feet, 'that would add to our woes. But I must be getting on my way now. I have other places to visit in the day. It might be best if you did not tell others about my visit.'

'Of course not, Alderman,' replied Francis sweetly, knowing perfectly well half the village had seen Henry arrive. 'Thank you for the courtesy of your call.'

'Clump, clump, clump.' Alderman Webster walked out even more aggressively than the way he came, almost tripping over Peebee as he left.

Chapter 8
Eleanor Is Touched

Eleanor Montagu busied herself in front of the mirror and applied her lipstick, a striking deep red, with great care. She had to be looking at her best at the Watermeadow party in the evening. She knew that buffoon, Frothy Watermeadow, would be announcing his purchase of the Hawton Six, and she wanted to be there to hear him talk about the gold. *'Poor fool,'* she said to herself, *'No wonder he is wallowing in debt. The aristocracy has lost touch with the financial levers that control our lives now. He seems to think that money is out there somewhere, and you just press a button to release it. He is hoping to press another button tonight, but this particular gambling machine is not going to deliver the jackpot.'*

She smiled to herself as she considered how much better informed she was than Frothy. This broadened into a self-satisfied girlish smirk when she contemplated the recent upheaval to her emotions. It first happened, quite when she least expected it, only a week ago. She was sitting in her office in Newark with Rock. He was normally very proper and business-like when discussing the plans for the gold that he had found to the east of the Watermeadow Estate. As the legal representative for the estate, Eleanor was there to offer her opinions and advice and found it so much easier talking to Rock than to Frothy. Rock at least knew what was going on, and it was such a pleasure talking to him than explaining every sentence three times over when she talked to Frothy. 'Could you say that again, Eleanor, I am not sure of the difference between a bailor and a bailee when it comes to gold; I just cannot stop thinking of people bailing water – tossing it here and there as they are panning for gold, I suppose.'

But on this particular day, Rock was clearly excited. He could not keep still, his voice was pitched differently, and he had a nervous cough. 'There's something else I need to tell you, Eleanor,' he said, suppressing a twitch of his lower jaw, 'I've discovered more gold than I expected, much more.' Eleanor sat forward, also excited.

'How do you mean? How much more?'

'I'm sorry to be a little mysterious, but I cannot tell you exactly; at least, not yet.'

'Why on earth not?'

It was then it happened. Both Eleanor and Rock were leaning forward with their arms resting in front on the table. Without saying anything, Rock gently moved his right hand across until it encountered Eleanor's own right hand, lightly brushing her forearm on the way. This was the first time they had ever touched, and Eleanor immediately felt a warm glow pass all the way up her arm and into her brain, where it exploded in a galaxy of ecstatic stars. So Rock really cared. He wasn't cold and distant; those little smiles and gentle compliments were real expressions of feeling. Here was a real man, and he cared, he genuinely cared.

She found it hard to release his grip and made it clear his feeling was reciprocated she crossed her left hand over to his, so they briefly looked as though they were playing an elaborate game.

But that was barely a week ago. In that time they had shared everything – their thoughts, their life histories, their innermost feelings, and their beds, and now had plans, very clear plans for the future. The thought of starting a new life with Rock reverberated inside her head like an excited metronome. Here was she, an ordinary solicitor from Newark, who found most people in the town a little beneath her and ever so slightly boring, about to share her life in the most amazing way with her rugged Adonis, seeing places she had never expected to visit, thrilling to anticipated pleasures she had hardly ever contemplated, and, so much more important, knowing that her income would remain disposable and she would be solvent for the rest of her days.

'Yes,' she said to herself, looking in the mirror, 'I really am 20 years younger. I am indeed what I feel.' She would definitely wow them this evening.

Chapter 9
King James Gets His Money

The morning of 20th April, 1603, in the village of Hawton was one that shouted gleefully to all, 'Spring is here at last!' As the sun rose over Balderton to the east and cast its long shadow of the church over the road and the field beyond, the wild flowers bursting forth completed the scene better than any painting. The white dead nettle in the may-blossomed hedgerows served as a backdrop for the showy primroses close by, the bugle with its stout shoots thrusting its purple-blue flowers through the dead leaves by the wood, and a carpet of daisies and buttercups highlighted the cowslips and oxslips nodding in the meadow. A tableau worthy of a king, never mind the villagers of Hawton. But, as it was perceived at a subliminal level every spring, it was largely unrecognized but unknowingly added to their general feeling of contentment.

The busy villagers were already hard at work. Geoffrey Walley, the stonemason, was improving the access to the church by creating smaller steps in the porch; Thomas Pryett, the dairy farmer, was milking the last of his cows for the royal party, pleased that the improved weather had almost doubled the yield in the past week; and David Cotter, the shepherd, was gathering his flock of 500 sheep to forage in the southern Newark marshes with Musket, his reliable collie, keeping them all in order. Young Harry Robertson was harnessing his horse to a cart to take the delectable creamy Hawton cheeses to Newark market, and Ann Calderdale, at the back of the rectory, was picking the last of her cabbages from her well-tended vegetable plot. 'I do hope the royal party will not need any more,' she muttered to herself as she picked them, 'If they do not leave soon, I will be quite distracted.'

But help would soon be forthcoming. King James looked out of the window of his comfortable bedroom at the House of Cordonnier at the bustling activities of the village. Gascon and his wife had been very good to him, even though they kept giving him pamphlets in French that he could barely understand.

There outside, Kim Chambers, the rector's cook, was serving out the last of the porridge to the royal party seated around the long table outside the church. She balanced the large pot expertly on her hip, and her ladle swung regularly like a metronome as each soldier was served in order.

Yes, James was happy in Hawton. He never expected to be, but he had been relieved of almost all responsibility while in the village. But important days loomed ahead. Soon he would be crowned King of England and Scotland. It would not be easy to join the two countries in harmony. He had the divine right to rule and that meant he was only accountable to God. But God might not always be there to advise him. Canon Ian Lambert, a very wise man of the cloth, had given him some good advice when he had visited a few days ago on his regular journey around the county. 'You might not always hear God,' he advised, 'but you must be always listening.'

James hoped He would be listening when he was trying to bring together the Scots and the English. The more he had seen of the villagers of Hawton, the more impressed he had become. These villagers seemed to be safe and secure in their lives; they did not squabble or argue, but got on with their tasks in good humour and with the minimum of fuss. And they did not harbour ill feeling. Harry Harmington, whose elbow was now better after it was found that his elbow was dislocated, not broken, had made friends with Jock McCaber, the soldier who had caused the injury, and they were now playing as partners on the expanding golf course to the north of the church, which even had a sand-pit made in one corner.

Some said it was called a bunker, but James thought that was a little odd for a game of movement.

He could not see this sort of bonhomie happening in his home country, where clans could be enemies for life. He had to admit, although it pained him deeply, that the villagers of England were more civilised. 'Ay,' he said to himself, 'reform, reform of the Scottish ruffians, ane heych purpose for a new king.' He would start at once.

A clattering of hooves disturbed James' musings. He looked through the window to see Rory Stewart circling the churchyard before dismounting from his horse. 'Guid,' said James to himself. 'He's got a sack wi' 'im. Booty frae the lairds, I hope.'

This was indeed the case. Rory had persuaded four of the landowners to give him gold and silver in coins and rings as advance payments for their knighthoods at Belvoir Castle. 'Dub the lot of 'em,' Rory said to James, 'Ye'll get yer money and their undying thanks; we all win.' King James could not but agree. For a man with an undying thirst for money, now he was king, the opportunities for further riches gleamed like seductive beacons ahead. So much for the winter of penny-pinching in Holyrood, now welcome the treasures of Westminster.

'Tell the soldiers we leave at noon, Rory. And mek sure we get some hounds to go wi' us for the hunting.' Now he had money, he could afford to spend and bringing hounds to Belvoir would show that he was beneficent. A charitable king must be more noble than a miserly one, and proper acknowledgement of his status could never be improved by penury. The only exception he could think of was Jesus Christ, and he had some advantages that even an English king did not possess.

But what about the people of Hawton? He and his men had stayed in the village for over a week and paid nothing. Did they deserve payment? He ruminated as he prepared to leave his room in the east wing of the Cordonnier household. In the distance he could see the rough sign advertising the work of Godfrey Hodgkin, the builder, meticulously arranging the stones for the walls of a new cottage, and thought of all the advantages of an uncomplicated life tight within the bounds of the village, with no need to be troubled by the wider world. Well, that was no option for a king. 'Get yer socks on, Jamie,' he said to himself, 'there's a country waiting for you to govern.' But he would not forget Hawton and its people, and they deserved something in reward. He would make sure by meeting Francis Clarke in the Rectory before he left.

Chapter 10
Steve Plays It Cool

Steve Pitchfork was not clever, but he worked hard at being cunning, and he sussed people up quickly. And today, on the day of the Watermeadow Party, he had reason to feel fairly satisfied with himself. To the hoity toities of Watermeadow he was just an under-gardener, with no aim in life apart from serving his masters, reliable but asinine, following orders even if they were stupid. This suited Steve greatly. He could touch his cap gratefully, apologise if anything went awry by saying, 'I'm just the gardener, and I just follow instructions.' So in this way he could stay out of trouble.

In his job as an under-gardener, he was in an excellent position to observe the people of the Watermeadow Estate. He always had jobs to do, and his knowledge of the grounds, their hidden coverts and spinneys, their spindly and fat hedges, the pockets among the yews where he could command a wide perspective but remain invisible himself, enabled him to listen in and observe almost all that was going on behind the walls of Watermeadow House. This would have amazed other people as very odd, as his status was such that he had hardly ever been allowed inside.

Steve also realised he was attractive to women. He could not quite work out why, because his mum and dad had never regarded him as handsome and just called him a twisted git, a term which was obviously just abuse and not designed to inspire self-confidence. But later, from the age of 16 onwards, he had the girls of Watermeadow, Hawton, Staunton and Cotham falling over themselves to share his company and, with the obvious intention of the more determined suitors, his life.

He did not reciprocate these feelings because he felt curiously detached. He liked young men and young women equally, but the thought of sex with either of them was largely theoretical. He could envisage, and even practise, it, but it did not really involve him emotionally. At times he thought there might be something wrong with him, but he could see advantages in being short on passion. It allowed him to be clear-headed when all around were confused and crazy. As for Lady Delta, she had been a godsend. Ever since that first kiss by the raspberry canes, she had searched him out whenever she was free. She had opened his eyes to the empty life of the Watermeadow crowd, the endless small talk, the tedious whist parties, the games of croquet on the main lawn that put everybody into terrible moods, the little snobberies that prevented any form of meaningful relationship with "the common people", or as they were more frequently called, "the others".

So he understood Delta's frustrations, and her wish to be free of all these pettifogging restrictions in her life. So when she spoke to him about the gold, the light of escape was in her eyes. She came to him, down by the large compost heaps, in a state of great excitement. 'You won't believe it, Steve, but Rock has found gold – somewhere on the estate but I don't know where – because I heard him talking to Eleanor. They were in Rock's shed. I was outside by the tall beech hedge – the one you've sculpted so nicely – and heard Eleanor shout "Is it really gold?" I could not hear much else apart from Rock shushing her and saying something like "Don't let on". But it must be true. We've suspected this for years, now we know.' They embraced, both trying to suppress the sweet decaying odour of the compost from their minds as they thought only about the precious metal that could change their lives.

Chapter 11
King James Leaves for Belvoir

It was time to leave Hawton. The last round of golf had been played, the tents had all been rolled up and packed away, the horses were saddled up and ready to go. The king's carriage was also ready, but its occupant was not. He had one more task to perform before he left Hawton.

Francis Clarke was preparing himself for his pastoral visits and was just putting his boots on when there was a knock on the door. He twisted and staggered a little as he shuffled his other foot into the bottom of the second boot. He must be fully in control when he answered the door. When he opened it, he was pleased he was now sure-footed; it was King James.

'Come in, Your Highness, what is your pleasure?'

'Rector Francis, you and the folk at Hawton have been very guid to me and my men.'

Francis was embarrassed.

'It was nothing. We were only too pleased to be your hosts. A minister of God has an obligation to receive visitors, whoever they may be. A royal one is no different, but, if I may be permitted to point out, a parson's reputation is made by the number of important people who stay in his parish. So a travelling king under my roof puts me in very good stead with the Diocese. In any case, we have been privileged to have you.'

King James smiled.

'Ye are too kind. But something amazes me. Ye have neither asked for gold or silver at any time. Your generosity shames a Scotsman like mysel'.'

'Money is of small import to us in Hawton. Our needs are modest, our income small, but we avoid debt, work hard and praise the Lord for his munificence.'

'Well, I think the Lord might need just a little assistance,' said James, bringing out a small leather purse from his top pocket. 'Here are three sovereigns for your hospitality for the past two weeks, as you've done so weel for me an' my men.'

Francis was overwhelmed. 'You are just too kind, Your Highness. We did not ask for, and did not expect, anything to be at your service. Our aim is to make generosity in Hawton an ever-present persuasion. But I must not act as the conscience of the village. There are those amongst us who have occasionally grumbled a little, just a little, and who would be very pleased to have extra resources for spring planting – so I hope you can trust me to distribute the money accordingly.'

'Of course, Rector, as ye weel. And now we must be off to Belvoir, and then to London. And when I arrive in Westminster, I promise, we'll tak' a cup o' kindness to all in Hawton for what ye've done. I now feel ready for all the tasks ahead.'

James turned on his heels and was swiftly gone. Francis looked out to see him climb into his carriage and call the Hawton hounds to heel. The entourage was complete, and Francis walked out of the Rectory to wave goodbye. He watched it slowly leave down the road to Cotham and the south, and when the last horse had disappeared, he wiped a tear from his eye.

On the bumpy road south, King James had time to think. His stay in Hawton had taught him a great deal. He had been in an oasis of calm and good nature for a whole two weeks and had seen no sign of conflict or division. The squabbling and intrigue of Holyrood was behind him, and he must learn to govern the two nations in a different way to his predecessors. War and victory, as his famous aunt, Queen

47

Elizabeth, had demonstrated, was highly popular, but was this the right way forward now?

The trouble was, wars were expensive, and if you did not win, you became very unpopular. He well remembered the teachings of his youth and the degree to which his predecessor, King John, had been hated 400 years ago. *He could not stop fighting battles and making enemies*, James reflected, *and I must not go down that bloody path again*. He must bring his peoples together. What was the word that was flickering at the back of his brain? "Consensus", that was it. If he governed with consensus, he would be on the right track. But he also had the divine right to rule, and how did this square with consensus, the idea of all working together? So this was going to be a tricky combination, but one that was worth thinking about. A new thought indeed, one that he had never considered as King of Scotland, so the stay in Hawton had been of great value.

As his carriage turned the corner to enter the village of Staunton, King James nodded off to sleep, with a smile that some might have thought was a smirk of self-satisfaction, but was really just one of contentment.

Chapter 12
Chris Challis Surveys His World

Chris Challis stood on the Mound in front of the Watermeadow Estate and looked down towards Prinny's Folly, the covert in the distance. He marvelled at the view, not as an artist might look at a painting, but as a surveyor, recognising and marking in his mind each clump of trees, each undulating grassy valley, and each stream channelled so perfectly towards the lake and its memorable arched bridge. This was his creation, and it must remain unchanged – indefinitely. Chris's luminary was Lancelot 'Capability' Brown, the architect who changed the face of country gardens 200 years ago, and altered attitudes forever. Chris had been fascinated by Lancelot Brown ever since he was an under-gardener at Burghley House near Stamford. After surveying each garden on horseback, Lancelot Brown decided on the "capability" of each estate, and had the vision to put it into practice. Chris had visited most of the gardens in the Midlands that Capability Brown had designed – Chatsworth, Belvoir Castle, Brocklesby Park, Burghley House, Charlecote, Coombe Abbey, Packington Park, and admired them all. When he came to the Watermeadow Estate as head gardener, he insisted on an additional title, that of landscape gardener.

This allowed him to put Lancelot Brown's ideas into his own practice, and his repeated references to his mentor gained him the title of "Capability Challis" very quickly. By having such an illustrious predecessor to quote from, Chris was able to get Frothy's agreement to many changes that he would otherwise have been reluctant to grant.

The first of these was inspired by Chris's visit to Chatsworth House. It was all very well having a magnificent panorama but you had to see it properly. The Watermeadow Estate was as flat as a pancake, so the only option was to construct a hill. This was the beginning of The Mound, the 40-ft colline far enough from the house not to obstruct the light, but close enough to command a view of most of the estate. There was great merriment among the estate workers when the Mound was proposed, but much cursing and grumbling when they had to start shovelling and digging. Chris sent them off to see the Civil War battlements at the Sconce in Newark, saying, 'If this was done 300 years ago in the middle of a war with disease everywhere, you should be pleased you're in the 20th century with modern tools.'

'Modern tools indeed,' said Steve Pitchfork, 'one clapped out Massey Ferguson tractor is all we've got, like an old man with a dodgy heart that keeps collapsing and needs intensive care before it can start up again.'

But the Mound took shape and before long, when each of the large Watermeadow family stood on its summit and saw the rest of the estate stretching out below, nobody could deny that it was a magnificent vista. But Chris had only just started on his capability journey. The marshy land by Prinny's Folly was partly drained, followed by the construction of a lake by damming a tributary of the River Devon, the addition of the arched bridge that beautifully caught the light of the setting sun, when everyone agreed 'it simply glowed', and the planting of yews, cedars, poplars and beech trees in thick stands and rows. He made sure the rows of trees pointed towards the distance in serried ranks like an army glorying in the exhibition of its power. All these features could be seen from the Mound, and Chris had ensured that the perspective was changed to such an extent that the distant boundary of the estate appeared to be far, far away, so adding to the panorama.

But on this afternoon of 3rd July, Chris was intensely concerned about the future of this great enterprise. Only a few days before Frothy had asked to see him in his study, a rare event.

'Chris, I want to tell you something in absolute confidence. Rock has discovered gold over to the east of the estate. I have not yet told the others as I am a great believer in surprises, what-ho, but I will be announcing it at my party on 1st July.'

'Then, excuse me, Lord Watermeadow, why are you telling me now?'

'Well, I've always tried to keep you in the picture as you are such an important part of our estate family. I felt I needed to tell you that there may be mining activity, if I can put it that way, to take full advantage of the discovery.'

'Sorry, Lord Watermeadow, I still don't see how that will affect me.'

'I'll come straight to the point, Chris, we may have to alter some of the landscaping that you have so diligently constructed. There is no access to the mining area except through the estate, and there may be some digging and erecting of mine shafts.'

Chris was flabbergasted. 'I'm sorry, but this is ridiculous. Lord Watermeadow, are you telling me that all my work, all my planning, all my sweating and toiling, all my efforts to make what I thought was your pride and joy, the Watermeadow Estate, into the jewel of the East Midlands, is going to be destroyed because of some damned stupid mine? Please excuse my language, but I cannot tolerate such a suggestion.'

'There is no need to get aerated, Chris. It all depends on Rock. At present he feels the gold can only be mined adequately from above. I am sure this can be done with the minimum of disruption.'

'I am not sure if you quite understand what this will mean, Lord Watermeadow. Do you really want your lovely estate to be made into a quagmire of mud and mire, to destroy a garden landscape that has taken 20 years to build, all for the sake of some measly lumps of metal? You may gain today, but tomorrow everyone will suffer.'

'Tush, tush, Chris. You are being melodramatic. It is not like you to make speeches more in keeping with politics than

51

with gardening. I am sure we can work out something that will meet with your approval.'

Chris felt ready to explode at this self-satisfied nincompoop who clearly had no understanding of the heritage and continuity of his estate, who could not see further than the pound signs dazzling in front of his eyes, and who saw Rock Solid as the means for his salvation. Something needed to be done to prevent this outrage. Still standing on the Mound, Chris scratched his head while he thought about a solution.

Chapter 13

Francis Receives a Sack, and Makes a Decision

Francis Clarke was carefully working out the best proportions of the three sovereigns to dispense to the villagers of Hawton. '94 villagers,' he muttered, 'in 29 households. Do I give the money to each family, or each household?' Francis was fastidious in financial matters; they were the source of much trouble if they went wrong. Even a misplaced farthing could lead to feelings of great injustice. Mrs Greenslade in the far cottage still grumbled that he had left her a halfpenny short when he was handing out the proceeds of the Church Christmas fair. In the end, he decided to give a shilling to each household, three shillings to Gascon Cordonnier as he had incurred most expense by looking after the king, and four for the Rectory, that was only fair.

He was interrupted by the thudding of hooves. He looked out of the window to see a burly man dismounting from a pony that was sweating badly.

'Another sack for the king,' said the bearded horseman. 'Message here,' he added, handing over a sealed bag.

He was clearly not a man of many words, so Francis allowed him to leave before breaking the seal and reading the message. 'Treasure for King James – and then, in smaller lettering, "abscondere faciam confidenter; non aperire".' Francis was not a Latin scholar but easily knew the words. 'Hide safely, do not open', he repeated to himself.

But what was he to do? The sack must be important – and valuable – but he had no idea when it would be reclaimed.

Francis Clarke then made one of the most important decisions of his life. He would bury the sack. *Did I really think that?* he startled himself by his daring, quite unbecoming of a quiet country parson, whose last major decision was to adjudicate the best position for Benjamin Harrow's gravestone in the churchyard, meticulously planned by Ben himself 15 years before he died, as he needed certainty in both life and death. But the option of burying the sack, however strange, was the only sensible one. He needed it to be secure, away from the villagers, the highwaymen, Alderman Webster and the grabbers of Newark, and from all the plotters in the realm, for there was much talk of sedition. King James could not count himself as secure. He had not yet been crowned, and there were always pretenders hovering round the throne, waiting for an opening.

Now Francis had made the decision many other questions flooded into his mind. Whom could he tell safely? Where should the sack be buried? How would he know the rightful owner? In the end, he decided to keep everything to himself. He would bury the sack after midnight and mark out its position on the church wall of the church using a code. Good. He would keep the code and its meaning in his safe box at home and would only disclose this to the emissary from King James.

So Francis only had to wait until dark to carry out his plan. He put the sack in the shoe box by the stove and covered it up. He felt a curious mixture of exhilaration and fear that he had never known before. 1603 was going to be a special year for him and the Rectory at Hawton.

Chapter 14
The Party Is Imminent

As the guests walked down Watermeadow Drive on 3rd July, the summer's day was heavy with fascinated expectation. Of course, the scientists will tell you that this must be nonsense, but were the flocks of starlings whirling away from the poplars more excited than usual, and did not the blackbirds scuttle across the lawns that little bit faster, and could you swear the squirrels swinging from the sycamores had no extra urgency? Was it the weather, which was cool for early July, or was it that so many of the guests were conspirators, hiding most of their thoughts and feelings from others, with plans that could determine the course of their lives?

Lady Delta was the first of the household to arrive. Lady Delta fancied herself as a singer, and loved the word "artiste" sometimes attached to her by those who wished to flatter. It was so exotic, and so un-Watermeadow, a place whose drab attempt to be stately made it less so. She had organised a musical ensemble, a vehicle to help convince the many visitors that she had genuine talent. Her friend Colin Doverman led the ensemble and as his piano playing was so fantastic, any minor errors on her part would pass unnoticed.

Colin arrived with Delta, together with the other players, and repaired to the drawing room to rehearse. Now the creditors of the Watermeadow Estate were also arriving. Frothy used to think of many of them as hyenas, waiting to feast on the Watermeadow corpse before it had even died, but today his perception was very different. There was friendly Robert Darlington, the manager of the Midland Bank, who had repeatedly saved him from penury by adjusting loans and invoices after Frothy had hoarsely told him, 'I cannot pay.' But Robert was never a hyena. Today this encapsulation of generosity in human form was a jolly Mr Pickwick, smiling broadly and greeting everybody cheerily as they travelled down the drive. 1948 was not a very good year for credit, but Robert stretched it to the limit, as many people were in his debt – literally, emotionally and professionally – as he had averted much financial scandal. Less attractive were the lenders from the companies linked to the Rotary Club, who had become increasingly irritable with Frothy's excuses over the months, but who today were now seen as affable hippopotamuses and rhinos, whom he could envisage as rolling over with fat smiles on their faces when he told them about the gold.

Steve Pitchfork was in the group too, but in his rarely worn, somewhat ill-fitting suit, he stood apart from the others, not that he minded, as he had much on his mind that he wanted to be kept there. He overtook Chris Challis, who was equally preoccupied, and after acknowledging each other by a brief nod, continued their solitary walks to the large front door. Eleanor Montagu was waiting in the porch, being fussed over by Emmy, the housemaid, and looking even more striking than usual. Her haughty smile to the two gardeners told more about her views on social status than any words could have done.

The Reverend David Milliner, the ostensible reason for the party, had also arrived with his wife, Augustina. They were in a particularly jolly mood, as they could look ahead to a life of at least partial retirement after looking after five churches in the past six years. This was akin to chasing a runaway train but never quite catching it. Although the congregations were on his side, the Diocese never seemed to be, and he was persistently arguing that the parish share demanded was ludicrously high. As so many of the churches needed repairs, and these were the responsibility of the church councils, not the Diocese, these extra demands seemed insensitive and unfair. But all these thoughts now seemed petty and uncharitable, and both he and Augustina were determined tonight to have a jolly good time.

Inside everything was buzzing. 'People who attend grand parties have scant idea of the organisation involved.' Maggie Carpenter was reminded of these words as she fluttered round the kitchen, jumping from place to place like a hen desperate to lay an egg in a hidden corner. Were the ovens at the right temperature for the beef, was the soup properly seasoned, had the right number of places been set for the visitors, and what would she do if any of the guests brought children? That would be a disaster in waiting.

She checked the guest list again. Forty-six of them were coming, with about five or six needing special succour because of their sensitive constitutions. Maggie and Lady Aqua often laughed together about catering for these fussy souls, who seemed to regard eating as a complex chemistry experiment, with exactly the right combination of strange foods to satisfy the most special of palates. It seemed from their insistent concerns that the wrong food could cause them to dissolve, explode or disintegrate entirely.

Fortunately, Maggie had Emmy to assist her preparations. Emmy lived nearby and was an absolute hive of energy. If you gave her a task to do, she would rush off, almost before you had finished a sentence, and within a few minutes she would be back for more instructions. She was like a coiled spring, waiting to jump up and unwind, and never seemed to tire. But if kept inactive, with nothing to do, she became irritable and edgy, and was critical of others who did not have her unbounded energy. The other staff at Watermeadow House found her a little difficult, and she quickly acquired the nickname of Her Emitense, a term that Emmy occasionally heard, but as she perceived it slightly differently, she felt mildly flattered. But Aqua recognised that Emmy was a person for big occasions only; then she was in her element.

Emmy had arrived in time to help. Aqua was relieved. 'Good for you, Emmy, you know the drill. It's one of those new buffets tonight. Everything out on the big table in the dining room, and no chairs to block people off. It's the special plates and bowls…'

As usual, Aqua hardly had time to finish the sentence before Emmy was on her way. She made her way to the large cupboard where all the Watermeadow crockery was kept, its resplendent flowery "W" pattern snaking round the perimeter of each dish, bowl and plate. This was one of the Watermeadow treasures that had not been sold to pay off debts, and Aqua was so pleased that their sale was now no longer on the agenda.

Within minutes, Emmy was back. Aqua now had time to complete her instructions. 'Lay the table for 60, Emmy. All the staff are coming as well.' Off Emmy flew again. Aqua was not quite sure that all the staff should be invited too but Frothy had insisted on it. 'Does the rabbits good to see the dogs occasionally,' he replied to her concerns, perhaps not realising that his comment indicated more condescension than generosity. But he was really more interested in making sure that everybody would know his news at first hand. There had been much gossip, and once he had made everything clear, at least this would become accurate.

Maggie and Emmy liked the music in the background as they shimmied and skittered round the house, and even though the peeling wallpaper and damaged skirting boards could not be hidden entirely, Watermeadow was indeed looking up.

Chapter 15
Francis Carries Out an Interment

Francis had arranged for his unlikely task to be carried out on a fine night with a moon nearly on the full. Eventually, the showers of April settled to give fine tranquil days. On the evening of 26th April, Francis was ready. The moon was as full as it would ever be, there was barely a cloud in the evening sky, and the village of Hawton was fast asleep. Just after midnight, Francis left the Rectory with a spade, and the precious sack, in a wheelbarrow. If interrupted, he would say he was burying a lamb far away from its short life on the meadow so that the foxes would be diverted from their nightly raids.

But nobody was there. Francis made his way slowly to the east along the path towards the village of Balderton. After a few yards, he left to join the South Willows Meadow.

Somewhere near the border of the wood, watched curiously by the sheep in the meadow, clustered together as though receiving tuition from moles, Francis drove his spade into the light clay soil and removed the upper turf. When he had excavated to a depth of five feet, he cleared the loose soil and placed the sack at the base. He replaced the rest of the soil and finally, covered the bare earth with the turf he had set aside. After treading in the turf carefully, he walked around the burial site, looking at it from all angles to see if it was truly concealed. He was used to conspicuous burials, not inconspicuous ones, so here he was a novice. A tawny owl hooted its apparent approval from the nearby wood, and Francis felt reassured.

He picked up his spade and wheelbarrow and made his way directly to Hawton Church, silhouetted like a sentinel in the middle distance. 'One, two, three...seven, eight, nine, ten,' Francis counted carefully with each step of the wheelbarrow. He continued counting right up to the church porch. 'Four hundred and ninety-eight, four hundred and ninety-nine.' He stopped.

He was now at the church and had almost completed his appointed assignment. Two parts remained, and Peebee the cat decided he should witness these. Francis lit a candle and walked down the nave. Then he drew a small knife from his breast pocket and carefully carved 'ID' on one of the walls, or was it 'Id'; it was difficult to be sure in the dark. Next to it he added an arrow pointing to the east and fashioned a sculp of his face (he had always wanted to add to the magnificent carvings in the church, and here at last was his opportunity). After finishing, he leant back and looked at the carving in the flickering light of the candle. He was really quite pleased by his modest effort and carving. 'That face really does look like me, it will show the way,' he said to himself. 'Whoever goes 499 yards directly to the east of the church will find the buried sack. The finder will have to work at it but I have given enough clues.'

Finally, he wrote, very carefully and deliberately, on some parchment close by, *'James lapides sacculi occultatum, inveniet faciem meam.'* He folded it and placed it in a small goatskin bag, and placed it in the stone safe in the back of the tower. He would be reminded of this whenever James' messenger returned. And if the messenger came back after Francis' death, God willing but please not too soon, there was enough information in the church to show where the sack was buried.

Francis felt his night's work had been a definite success. He snuffed out the candle, locked the church carefully after ensuring Peebee was safe in the tower, and walked back to the Rectory. As he quietly changed into his nightclothes, he was pleased to note that Matilda was still sleeping soundly, even thought she was lying on her back and was reverberating with her usual troubling snores when in this position. But, never mind, he would now sleep well, no matter what the interruptions may be. His worrying task was now over; he could return to be a respectable Rector again.

Chapter 16
Toast to the Vicar

It was half-past six. Everyone had now arrived. The last of the visitors was Arthur Mansfield, a detective inspector with the Nottinghamshire Constabulary. Arthur was well-known to the family. He had started work as a bobby in Farndon and Hawton soon after leaving school, and it was soon clear to all that he would be promoted. He had an analytical brain, and, as a fan of Sherlock Holmes, believed fully in the value of evidence. Even as an ordinary police constable, he had shown these special abilities.

The villages were peaceful places in the years before the war, when far away everyone was talking about or practising aggression, but there were occasional miscreants. One persistent burglar was eventually unmasked by Arthur. He escaped from a cottage window in a hurry one night but left one of his boots behind. Arthur examined the boot closely and noticed the sand grains in the sole were not local but came from a nearby quarry. He concluded the burglar must have worked in the quarry and visited there incognito. It was not long before a young man was seen working there with shiny new boots. Arthur took his fingerprints; they matched those in the burgled house and two others in the village. A confession soon followed.

So nobody was surprised when Arthur was promoted to detective constable and later to inspector. His promotion was acclaimed at Watermeadow, and he was invited most years to tell stories about crime in Nottingham, a town only a short distance away but light years away when it came to vice and violence. Arthur was scrupulous in his tales, disguising them greatly to avoid any disclosures of confidential data, but he need not have minded too much; everybody was uncritically fascinated to hear about gunshots in public parks, lorries with contraband goods and strange women in the night.

Frothy and Aqua had gathered all the guests together in the large drawing room at Watermeadow. Maggie and Emmy had muscled up all the champagne glasses from different places – it was unusual to have so many visitors – and although the glasses were of different shapes and sizes, they were undoubtedly meant for champagne, and this added novelty to each tray. Aqua also helped, putting some glasses aside for special guests.

From the music room the cadence of Delta singing her favourite song floated into the assembled visitors, adding a touch of romance and poignancy to the setting. Everyone was settling in well.

'That certain night
The night we met
There was magic abroad in the air
There were angels dining at the Ritz
And a nightingale sang in Berkeley Square
I may be right, I may be wrong
But I'm perfectly willing to swear
That when you turned and smiled at me
A nightingale sang in Berkeley Square.'

'Come in, you musicians,' called out Frothy. 'As you've put us in the mood for drinks, you deserve to have them.'

Delta, Colin and the ensemble came in with shining faces. Champagne, Moët et Chandon for most, but Taittinger when the Moët ran out, was distributed. Frothy beckoned David Milliner to the front of the guests

Frothy puffed himself out, but he was already a little puffy.

'We are very pleased to welcome you all to this special party at Watermeadow. I hope you are all in the mood for a party – I certainly am – and we have a lot to celebrate tonight. It is so good to see so many of you here from all walks of life. It shows we are a real community at Watermeadow. We treasure all, and I really do mean that sincerely. First, though, I would like, on behalf of you all, I am sure, to give a toast to our departing vicar, David, and his delectable wife, Augustina, as they leave our parish. David is moving on to the important post of chaplain to the Nottinghamshire Fire Service. So it's a case of out of the Hawton frying pan into the county fire, what ho, David?'

Frothy paused briefly for effect, and there was a dutiful titter.

'But although there are hot days ahead, we also have warm memories of their time here and all of us need to cherish the importance of their pastoral work in Watermeadow, Hawton and beyond. So, I ask you to raise your glasses and give three cheers to the pillar of our society, the Reverend David Milliner: hip, hip, hooray; hip hip hooray; hip, hip, hooray!'

The guests broke into applause and cries of 'speech, speech', from those who always shouted 'speech, speech' at these occasions, were directed at David. He was not quite expecting such a fulsome toast and was mildly embarrassed, but he forced himself to enter into the spirit of Frothy's occasion.

'I, and Augustina, are quite overwhelmed by this tribute, Frothy. After all, I am just a humble vicar and in serving God and the spiritual needs of this parish, I have only done what my predecessors have done here for 600 years. But, nonetheless, we are very moved by your thanks and good wishes, and only wish to make one correction. I have been doing my history homework in preparing for a dramatic production and have to remind you of the message of Magna Carta. "None so high as to be above the law" is a fundament of government, so the ultimate pillar of our little group is Arthur Mansfield here. It is he who ultimately keeps our society intact and for its values to be maintained.'

There was applause from all in the room, but those who clapped politely little knew how prophetic these words were to be.

Chapter 17
Rector Francis Clarke Nears His End

It was now October 1619, and Francis Clarke was dying. He had been confined to bed for over three months now, his appetite had almost disappeared, and he was beginning to get confused. Matilda had done all she could, exhorting him to eat and drink, and at first she convinced herself that it was only her unimaginative cooking that had sparked his decline. But now she understood. Francis was about to meet his Maker, and there was nothing she could do about it apart from making his final days as comfortable as she could.

But on this particular morning, Francis was a little more alert, if not actually agitated. After she had attempted to give him his favourite porridge topped with plum jam, she decided to desist further attempts after he had taken two mouthfuls and pushed it away. His eyes were brighter than usual, and he wanted to talk. His head was clear.

'Matilda, there is something you need to know before I pass on. I have to tell you, but I cannot advise you what to do.'

'You are talking in puzzles, Francis. What is it that is so important if it requires no action? Can it not be left to rest?'

Francis raised himself up in his bed.

'No, no, no, Matilda. I must tell you. I should have told you before, but never had the courage.'

'This is most unlike you, Francis, my love. We have always enjoyed the principle of sharing. What has happened to cause you to lapse?'

'Listen carefully, Matilda. This is not a time for the canker of criticism. You will remember the time King James left those sovereigns all those years ago.'

'Yes, only too well, my love. I would not want to go through that sharing process again. In the end, I do not think anyone was satisfied. I do not want to see people again wishing to split farthings in two. But you were amazing. St Peter at the pearly gates could not have been more patient or kinder.'

'Yes, yes,' interrupted Francis, 'but that was not the only treasure, if I can call it that, left by King James. Some days later, one of his horsemen delivered a sack of jewels, silver, or other objects – I never knew what was in the bag – but I was told to guard them until King James' men retrieved them. But when no one came, I felt I needed to hide them. I could not hide them here, with Alderman Webster and his men prowling around like urban highwaymen, so in the end, I buried them over in the South Willows Meadow, and, as far as I know, they are still there. I was expecting an emissary from King James' court, but nothing happened, and after 16 years, I think it has all been forgotten.'

'But what do you want me to do, Francis? Go out with a spade and dig it up?'

'That is the cause of my bother, Matilda. I honestly do not know what I want to do, or what I want you to do. I only know I have to tell you to relieve my burden. When you have a chance to discuss it with our sons, I am sure the right solution will be found.'

These last words were delivered more hesitantly, and Francis dropped back on his pillow with a loud sigh. Matilda, always observant as well as considerate, realized there was no useful purpose in asking more questions.

Later she sat in the front room of the rectory, poking the logs on the open fire, and pondered. Francis' revelations had troubled her, but she could quite understand why he had been quiet for so long. Buried treasure and the Hawton Rectory were strange bedfellows that could hardly be further apart. He had now passed on the responsibility of knowledge to her, and she must shoulder it as he had done. Men seldom shared these responsibilities with women, and even though she had realized long ago that she was just as capable as her husband, she was still proud that he had passed on his secret.

Still later, after a difficult supper when Francis again avoided eating, she made her decision. The treasure, or whatever it was, and it may just be a heap of old iron, should stay where it was. She would not ask Francis exactly where it was buried but would pass on to her sons, Joseph and Martin, the rumour that there was something important buried in the South Willows Meadow. If they, or any others, decided to look, they might find whatever was buried there, but would have no idea where it came from and how it arrived in the field. In this way, she and Francis could be exonerated of any responsibility once the treasure was found, if indeed it ever was.

The next morning she talked again to Francis again after more herculean attempts to persuade him to eat his porridge. He seemed uplifted, if that was the right word for someone who could barely rise from his bed.

'I feel so much better since telling you about the treasure, Matilda. I have no right to ask, but can you tell me what you have decided to do?'

'You can certainly ask, Francis. My answer is that you can set your mind at rest. A solution has been found, but there is no reason to disclose it to you. Fret not, and know that all will be well.'

Francis sank back into the bed again, with a smile gradually percolating across his face, and was soon in a deep sleep.

Chapter 18
Something Is Lying by the Pergola

'Thank you, all,' shouted Frothy, necessarily loudly as the dull peeling walls of Watermeadow House made acoustics poor, 'You are welcome to explore the house and gardens before the buffet in the dining room in half an hour. Remember then to pick up your plate and cutlery by the door and circulate around the grand table. You'll find it is a great experience.' This was one of the first times he had used the "buffet" word and by emphasising it as "boo-fay", he made it sound like a children's game, which of course to him it was.

Most people chose to move around the house rather than the garden, as it was still a little cool for early July, but the staff, who felt a little out of place in a crowd of what they perceived as stuffed shirts, took the opportunity of taking some fresh air. The evening was still, the blackbirds and thrushes were beginning their evensong, the surrounding trees stood in clean ordered lines as Chris Challis intended, and the visitors walked reverentially in silence through the glades, some still carrying their drinks, uncomfortably, as though they were all interlopers at a baronial ceremony.

Delta and Steve strode off together, always keen to spend their precious time away from others, Chris had to be outside so he could admire his arboreal creations in the dusk, and Rock too was nearby, deep in thought, still with a glass in his hand. Eleanor also was wanting to be alone with her excited thoughts and was sitting by the pond away from the others.

Inside, Aqua was nervously checking on the numbers of guests and calculating if there was enough food for them all.

Although in 1948 people could not expect to have all they wanted, it would be nothing short of disaster if there was not enough food at Watermeadow to go around. But the trouble with a buffet was that you could never compensate for sheer greed, and so she had organised reserve plates hidden in the kitchen with Maggie in case individual gluttony was seen to be sabotaging their plan. Emmy was setting out the cutlery, cleverly wrapped identically in serviettes as shown in the pages of Good Housekeeping open in front of her. She looked with pride at her finished tableau of rows of white feathers, each with silver necks exposed; this was definitely "classy", and she wished she had a camera.

The clock was ticking towards 7 o'clock and almost everything was ready. Maggie had a hot flush – she was at that time of life but why did they always come at the most inconvenient times – and just had to get out into the open air. She rushed out on to the south lawn and the cool of the evening served its expected correction. But what was that over by the pergola? Was it a large dog, or could it be a sheep that had escaped from the nearby meadow? She moved closer, curious, to investigate.

No, it was not an animal. It looked human. When she got closer, she realised it was Rock, apparently lying down. 'You really scared me, Rock. I thought you might be a sheep – but what on earth are you doing down there? Not prospecting again, I hope?'

Her words tailed off. There was no answer. Maggie looked more closely. Rock was not moving. He did not seem to be even breathing. This was too much. A wave of panic, much worse than a hot flush had ever been, broke over her, and she screamed, not just once but over and over again, as she ran back to the house faster than she had ever run before.

The guests had heard the screams. They flocked to the French windows and the kitchen door. Frothy and Aqua were nowhere to be seen. Fortunately, Arthur Mansfield was there to meet Maggie as she arrived, breathless, flushed and almost speechless.

'Rock,' she spluttered. 'Over there,' she pointed over to the pergola in the distance. 'Sorry, collapsed, might be done, awful'… She was close to incoherence, and Emmy shepherded her into the kitchen quickly and sat her down. Arthur and some of the other more mobile guests trotted towards the pergola, increasing their speed as they approached. By the time they arrived, Delta, Steve, Chris and Eleanor were also there looking nonplussed. Frothy and Aqua followed soon afterwards. Arthur quickly dropped to the lawn beside Rock, checked his pulse and breathing, rolled him on to his back and pushed rhythmically up and down upon his chest. 'Loosen his shirt, make sure his airway is clear. Someone get back the house and phone an ambulance.' Steve dropped down beside him and followed instructions. Arthur clearly knew his first-aid.

But after five minutes, they stopped their efforts. Rock was blue and lifeless; a stream of yellow mucus dribbled down his cheek. 'It's not too good,' said Arthur. 'Go back to the house and get the ambulance to come across the lawn here as soon as it arrives. We need to get Rock to hospital as a matter of emergency. The rest of you go back to the house. You may not feel like it but it is time for dinner, and we can sort everything out here.' Arthur wanted everyone to leave quickly. There was something very odd. He wanted to investigate the death without interruption – and there were distinct advantages in others being unaware that Rock was already dead.

Frothy and the others slowly tracked their way back to Watermeadow House. Other guests were now attracted by the fuss and were coming out of doors. 'What on earth is going on?' said Robert Darlington in his avuncular way, before his sensitive eyes and ears realised this was something serious and care was going to be needed.

'You heard what Arthur said,' Frothy muttered. 'This is a rum do, but we've got to make the best of it. Dinner is prepared and we might as well have it – we can't have it going to waste.'

It was a sombre procession that trooped into the dining room, all whispering amongst themselves and looking around furtively as conspirators do. Emmy, despite the unfortunate interruption, was still very proud of her serviette display and hoped by encouraging everyone to see it as they entered the dining room, they might be diverted. But they were not. The merriment of the occasion had been completely extinguished. What would be the reckoning?

Chapter 19
Arthur Takes Control

Arthur met the ambulance crew as they gingerly negotiated the south lawn to the pergola. He showed his police badge to them – how fortunate to have this on his person today, was it a sixth sense that had made him bring it with him at the last moment or just his natural tendency for order?

'Very sorry, but there's nothing more you can do for this man. His name is Rock Solid – yes, I know it's an odd name but that is what it is – and I understand he has no relatives here. Take him to the mortuary and let the attendants know the death might be suspicious; do not disturb anything. I need to speak to the pathologist before the post-mortem. Here are my details.' He handed out one of the little business cards he had just had cyclostyled in a publisher's, looking at it briefly first. 'Arthur Mansfield, Detective Chief Inspector' it read, with all his contact details. He sometimes found his title hard to believe and needed to be reminded of it. But if he really was a senior detective, he must act like one. The ambulance men knew quiet authority when they saw it and responded as Arthur had said.

As Arthur walked back slowly to Watermeadow House, he sensed the opportunity to find answers to Rock's death. That strange smell around his body, the absence of any bruises or injuries, the simple evidence that this was a man in the prime of his life a few minutes ago; this was not a natural death. And if it was an unnatural death, all the people who might know why were likely to be at the party. Who could they be? What motives for harming or killing Rock might they have? Whatever else happens, he must not let a potential suspect leave without being interviewed.

This was a tall order. He needed help. The answer suddenly came to him. Gilles Cordonnier used to help him as an interpreter at the lace industry in Nottingham when there were odd goings-on with French companies trying to obtain secrets from a dying trade. Gilles was French himself, and the family had alternated between living in France and England ever since the 16th century. He worked as the estate manager and financial controller of Watermeadow and knew everybody. Arthur also knew he could trust Gilles with his last farthing. Indeed, Gilles was so taken by the picture of the little wren on the back of each farthing, he took them back to France as birthday presents, and his nephew in Figeac had a collection for every year since 1937. So Gilles was well placed to be his assistant. But he must move fast.

When he came back into Watermeadow House, everything was confused. Most people were indeed in the dining room but their eating was desultory. Aqua and Maggie need not have worried about running out of food; only half of it was eaten and many plates had half-eaten beef, rabbit and potatoes, a rare sight for 1948. But the two family Labradors, Brunel and Kingdom, were waiting, wide-eyed, for their feast of the year. Arthur pushed past the guests and found Frothy and Gilles in a corner in deep conversation.

'I'm sorry to spoil things, Frothy, but could you ask everyone to meet in the hall? I need to make an announcement. And, whatever happens, do not allow anybody to leave.'

'Whatever for, Arthur? Can you please explain what is going on?' Frothy felt he was losing control of the situation, which of course he was, but as lord in his own manor, he could not tolerate playing second fiddle to a secondary figure like Arthur. A man in his position needed to be respected, not instructed.

'I will explain very shortly, Frothy, but action is needed now. Please do as I say. You will understand why within minutes.'

Frothy nodded irritably and went to tell Maggie and Aqua, before announcing Arthur's message. Arthur grabbed Gilles by the shoulder and moved him quickly toward the ante-room in the lobby. He closed the door and checked nobody was in earshot.

'Gilles, I do not have much time, but I want you to agree to help me. I have reason to believe that Rock's death was not an accident or other natural event. If I am right, it is very likely that some of the people here may know why. Before any of the people here leave, I want you and I to check them out to make sure they are above suspicion.'

'I am only too pleased to 'elp, Artour (he could never get the name quite right), but 'ow do I do this? And why do you zink it is me that can 'elp?'

'I will come to the point, Gilles. It is very likely that Rock was murdered. I know this sounds wild. I have no proof of this and do not want others to know that I think this might be true. What is imperative is that nobody who might know something about it should leave here without being questioned. As you know everybody here, or at least know much more than anybody else, I must have your help. I just cannot do it on my own.'

Gilles recognised the plaintive element. Arthur did need him. It was all very odd, but Arthur was a good man, and he could not let him down.

'Just tell me what to do, Artour, I will aid you. You can count on your ami, Gilles. C'est absolument oui. Il n y'a pas un problem.' When Gilles got emotional, he sometimes forgot his language.

Chapter 20
The Suspects Are Identified

Arthur and Gilles stood at the door as the Watermeadow guests filed past them into the dusk of the evening. Frothy had managed to create a plausible explanation for their additional scrutiny. They all knew that Rock had become seriously ill, although there was uncertainty about his actual death. Frothy had suggested he might have had a rare infectious disease and so a word was needed with everybody about their recent travels.

Gilles was in his element as the filterer-in-chief. Most of the people filing past were known to him. There was Mark Taylor with his wife, Beryl, the builder who lived down the unadopted lane in the village, and who helped all his neighbours without ever charging them. Then followed Dean Hythe, the former mayor, who supported every charity in the area; Robert Darlington, still, despite everything, displaying his encouraging smile and joie-de-vivre; and Jane Robinson, a well-known philanthropist with a penchant for water plants, who had stocked the Watermeadow pond with her favourite Acorus or sweet flag, as well as many other wetland species. No, there was no reason why any of these good people should be kept behind, so after a few words about their recent movements, they continued on their way, all still a little perplexed about an occasion that had gone badly off the rails.

On the other side of the passage was Arthur. He had no doubt about some of the suspects. He had known Rock for several years but had never been able to work him out. He seemed to have no allies, was secretive in both his movements and what he said, and often disappeared for days. He certainly had few friends, but who were his enemies? Gilles had not been able to help much. ''e as always been a mystery, like a book that ees always closed,' he told Arthur.

So Arthur had to guess a little. He took the obvious route of enquiry. Anyone who had been with, or had any sort of encounter with Rock, recently or in the past, should be interviewed in depth. Even if they were completely innocent, they could help to build up evidence. His training was coming useful. All detective work followed simple logic. So Frothy, Aqua, Delta and other members of Watermeadow House had to be seen. The gardeners and other staff in the estate also had to be included. And he had a few other clues from objects he had picked up from Rock's clothing that were of help. Eleanor Montagu was another who deserved an interview also.

By quarter to eight, everybody apart from the rump of possible suspects had left. These had been directed into the sitting room, where they sat, irritably, avoiding each other's gaze. They were giving the impression that someone in the room was indeed harbouring some highly infectious bug, but, in fact, all were nervously awaiting what revelations were coming next.

Arthur and Gilles entered. Frothy felt he had to say something. He often did so without realising that silence was a much better option, but nobody had ever had the courage to give him this most valuable advice.

'Well, Arthur. Sorry to make your day off into a busman's holiday. But, of course, you can leave it all till next week. After all, it is the weekend.'

'Sorry, Frothy. I need to put you into the picture and explain what I am doing,' replied Arthur. 'Rock has died under very strange circumstances. I want to ask all of you some questions to determine exactly what these circumstances were, and there are particular advantages in asking you these questions now. And because all of you are likely to be able to assist me, I do not want you to leave until I agree you can.'

'That is ridiculous,' cried Eleanor, who seemed more upset than the others about Rock's death. 'We have had a very trying day and need to get some rest.'

'I understand your feelings, Eleanor, but this is now a police investigation, and I cannot give you any choice.'

'Why on earth not? You are not suggesting that one of us might be responsible for Rock's death?'

'I am not suggesting anything. This is an investigation only, and I am here to try and find the truth. You are all my assistants in this task, even if you feel you have nothing to say that may be of value to me. I know you may feel I am wasting your time, but I assure you that even the smallest piece of information may be crucial.'

Frothy again judged things badly.

'I'm inclined to agree with Eleanor. It has been a difficult day, and we are all very tired. Cannot we leave it until another day at a better time?'

'I am sorry, Frothy. At least my first set of interviews will need to be done this evening. Some of you may not be needed again but others will. While all this is fresh in your minds, and also in mine, it will aid my task enormously if see you now. I also wish to see each of you separately and for you to be kept apart from all the others when you are not seeing me. Gilles will organise this, and I hope we can start immediately. I am not going to see you for long tonight, but will have to start again with some of you in the morning. Have any of you any further questions?'

This was enough to silence everybody. If Arthur was going to interview no matter what they said, it was best for this to start immediately.

'Good. I will start with Frothy, and after that, Aqua and Delta. Gilles will show the others to their waiting rooms.'

'Cor, this is getting really exciting,' said Emmy to Maggie, before they were separated by Gilles into different parts of the kitchen. 'I've been reading a book by this crime writer, Agatha Christie, and what's 'appening here is exactly what 'appens in her books. Makes me go all tingly.'

Chapter 21
Frothy Spills the Beans

Frothy, determined as always to appear to be in control, did not wait for Arthur to start his interview.

'Now look, Arthur, just for the sake of form, this isn't a formal criminal hoo-ha, is it?'

'I am not sure what you mean, Frothy,' said Arthur crisply. 'I am just trying to find out what happened. My inquiry may lead into criminal alley-ways, it may lead to somewhere quite innocent, or come to a dead end. I have no idea at this stage. But I must ask you to take this seriously, and be as accurate as possible in your replies.'

Frothy was chastened. 'All right, fire ahead.'

'I recall that you said you had a great deal to celebrate when you made the toast earlier this evening. What were you going to say, and had it anything to do with Rock?'

Frothy realised he had to come clean about the gold. It was bound to be disclosed anyway, but how different the circumstances!

'Well, it all seems such a long time ago, now, but I was going to announce an important discovery. Gold has been found on the Watermeadow Estate, and I was going to tell everybody about it.'

'Where exactly on the estate? In the grounds?'

'No. You may have heard. I have just purchased six acres to the east of the church, and the gold has been found in that area.'

'I am not going to pursue this now, Frothy, but did you know about the gold when you decided to make your purchase?'

'I do not choose to answer that question at the moment. And I suggest it is not relevant to your enquiry.' Frothy was not going to let Arthur take over completely.

'As you will, Frothy. But it may be relevant later. But, in the context of the gold, where does Rock come into it?'

'It was Rock who discovered the gold. You already know he is a geologist, and I gave him the job of looking for gold after all the rumours about it over the years. It was a long shot, but he came up trumps.'

Arthur wanted to move on quickly. Frothy was not easy to interview.

'So to be more precise, when did Rock find out about the gold, where is it now and who knew about the discovery?'

'Rock discovered the gold a few weeks ago, but I was not going to tell the others until this evening. I wanted it to be a surprise. Rock has given some of the gold to me for valuing but the rest, I understand, is still in the ground and will need to be mined.'

'And just exactly was your relationship with Rock?'

Frothy paused and swallowed slightly.

'Well, he was not a man who said more than was necessary.'

'What exactly do you mean by that?'

'You know, kept his cards close to his chest.'

'Did you trust him?'

Frothy was getting flustered. 'Mm, about as much as you can trust anyone nowadays.'

'So the reason you bought the land was to ensure that the gold was on your property when it was officially discovered?'

'I suppose you could say that.'

'I don't suppose – that was the reason, wasn't it?'

'Yes.'

'And what arrangement had you come to with Rock over what we might call 'the proceeds' of the gold transaction?'

'Erm, well, not really definite, we said at the beginning that he would get 40%.'

'That seems quite generous. Who actually picked on the figure of 40%?'

'It was Rock – for as he said, but for him there would have been no gold. It was his discovery.'

'But did you agree that 40% was the right figure?'

Frothy was now sweating a little. 'I was hoping for a slightly smaller proportion for Rock, as I have been paying him all this time.'

'So to clarify, Frothy, you and Rock, only, knew about the gold and had made an agreement to pay him 40% of the proceeds.'

'Well, it is a little more complicated than that.'

'That is all, Frothy, for the moment. I have quite a few interviews and will probably see you again in the morning.'

Chapter 22
Maggie Fills in Some Details

Arthur decided to see Maggie next. She seemed to be the eyes and ears of Watermeadow, and she would be much easier to interview than Frothy.

She came in from the kitchen and sat down in the comfortable chair with its high back and impressive floral decorations. It felt good to be sitting in a chair normally reserved for Frothy and Aqua. But she was keen on this interview, not the comfort of the chair, and sat forward expectantly. Arthur could see immediately that here was someone who had nothing to hide.

'I hope you can help me to piece bits of a jigsaw for me, Maggie. First of all, can you tell me if you know anything about gold in the Watermeadow Estate?'

'Oh yes, I can. It's been one of those strange subjects for weeks here. Strange, because everyone seems to know about it but not want to talk about it in the open.'

'If you had to summarise it, Maggie, what was known and who knew it?'

Maggie frowned in concentration; she wanted to be accurate. After all, the characters in Agatha Christie novels were always very clear in their statements, even if they were telling lies, and she wanted to be equally clear but truthful.

'I want to help you, Arthur, but I also do not want to appear disloyal. It all really started when Frothy and Aqua (I don't want to be rude but hope you don't mind me using their first names) were talking about buying the Hawton Six – the extra six acres to the east of the village. We all knew that

Frothy was not well off, to put it mildly, so could not understand why he wanted to spend money on this agricultural land when it came up for sale. After all, Frothy isn't a farmer. He can't tell the back-end of a horse from a sheep, so why would he want this land? Then we heard that Rock had been making tunnels on the east of the property. He pretended that it was all concerned with understanding and improving the soil, but this did not really make sense.'

'But where did the idea of gold come from?'

'It's always been around for years in this part of the world. So when people thought about what Rock was doing, and then seeing that Frothy was looking more and more pleased, these two, plus the buying of the Hawton Six, all suddenly clicked. These were all connected and the likely answer was that gold had been found. So the gossip got around that gold had been found in the Hawton Six. Nobody was sure, but when Rock was challenged about it, he wouldn't answer but looked guilty – he never could hide his feelings – so it all seemed to be confirmed.'

'Have you any idea who knew about the gold definitely, and who just suspected it?'

'Well, Rock, of course, must have known. And he has been spending a lot of time with Eleanor – I think she was a bit soft on him – and, if there was gold around, as the family solicitor, she would need to know about it too. And Frothy cannot keep a secret very well – although I do want to say he's a very nice man – so I suspect that Aqua and Delta were in the picture as well. I'm not sure about the others. Steve and Chris in the gardens must have seen what Rock was doing and asked questions, and it is very hard to think that they didn't know about it too.'

'That is very helpful, Maggie. And what about the staff in the house? Did they know about the gold?'

Maggie laughed.

'No, we were the ones always kept in the dark, so we just became the gossip crowd. We reported back on what we had seen or heard when we had a spare moment but it was all gossip. There was some talk about Delta and Steve, the under-gardener, as they were seeing an awful lot of each other, and someone once heard the word "gold" in their conversation, but that's about as far as it went.'

'And how did everybody get on with Rock?'

'Now that is really difficult. Rock was a loner, and nobody really knew what he was like, except perhaps Eleanor, and so we all kept our distance. I don't want to do your job for you, Mr Mansfield, but you probably noticed when it was announced that Rock was seriously ill, nobody was really upset. That's because although he had been working here for a long time, he always seemed to be on the outside.'

'I know this is a difficult question to answer, Maggie, but can you think of anyone who might be very happy if Rock was no longer alive?'

Maggie noted he had not used the word 'murder'. She guessed it was because he did not want to upset her, but it would have been nice for him to know that she could have dealt with it perfectly well.

'That is certainly a difficult one. I can't really say, but if all this has something to do with the gold, then a lot of people might be pleased. I have no idea of the financial arrangements in the household, but if Rock had found gold, as we all suspected, we knew he must have a lot of say in what happened to it. If he was no longer around, it would make everything simpler for a lot of people.'

'As I thought, Maggie. That has been a very useful interview indeed. I now feel I no longer wish to see Emmy, but I will have to see the others. Could you please make sure they stay in their rooms until I need them? First of all, could you see Gilles and ask him to invite Aqua to come in, and, please, do not talk about our interview with anyone for the time being.'

Maggie left, tingling with pleasure. She had performed well as the detective's assistant. Agatha Christie would have been proud of her. But she must follow Arthur's instruction. There must be no gossiping, no interfering with the inquiry. She might be needed to help Arthur again.

Chapter 23
Aqua Gets Distressed

Aqua was flushed and emotional as she entered the interview room. Her hair was a mess and she felt frumpy. This was not the message she wanted to give to Arthur. As the lady of the house, she had to act like one. She sat upright in the high-backed chair and tried to look in control.

'I hope I will not need to keep you too long, Aqua,' said Arthur, kindly, as he recognised some signs of distress, 'but there are just a few questions that I would like to ask. First, and quite importantly, did you know about the gold that had been found to the east of the estate?'

'Not really, but I guessed something was going on.'

'Come off it, Aqua. I cannot accept that as an honest reply. You knew all about the family's financial difficulties, and Frothy has told me what he was planning to say later in the evening. I cannot believe that Frothy kept you in the dark about his discovery of the gold.'

Aqua could see that Arthur would no longer tolerate evasion. She had to be clearer.

'Well, I did know that Rock had found something of value in his excavations, and I thought it was probably gold in view of all the gossip that has been around for years. But I had no idea how much it was and whether it was significant.'

'But you must have known it was just an odd flake or two. You must have had some indication from Frothy that its value was substantial.'

'Yes, Frothy was pretty excited about it all when he told me. He said it would solve all our financial problems.'

'And you must have known about this before he bought the Hawton Six; otherwise, the purchase would have seemed nonsensical.'

'I am not sure if I agree with "nonsensical", but Frothy told me about this when I questioned him about the purchase. We did not really need more land.'

Arthur breathed a sigh, not quite of satisfaction, but one indicating a signpost of progress.

'Moving on, what did you think of Rock?'

'I'm a generous person and like to get on with people, but I have to say I always thought he was a bit shady, never letting on about anything.'

'So it would be fair to conclude you were not exactly friends.'

Aqua nodded.

'Now I could not help noticing, Aqua, that the champagne glasses you produced at the reception were all of different shapes. Was there any particular reason for that?'

This irritated Aqua. It was clear Arthur had no breeding.

'Of course. A fine house should engender distinction. One of our distinguishing glassware features is that every champagne glass is different from every other.'

'I appreciate that. But this also means that you could identify each glass and give it, should I say, to the appropriate person.'

'I am not exactly sure what you mean by that remark.' Aqua could feel a wave of anxiety rising inside her.

'It may be completely unimportant, but I also could not help noticing that you helped to pour the drinks, so you could direct them to the right people accordingly.'

Aqua now lost control altogether. She burst into tears.

'I have no idea what you mean by that accusation, that terrible slur. I was just doing my best to help, to try and make the party go well. I cannot tolerate…' She broke off, her voice breaking.

'I am not making any accusation, Aqua, and I apologise if I have upset you. That is the end of our interview for this evening. You are at liberty to go now, and I do appreciate that this must have been a very difficult day, especially when at the beginning, expectations were so high.'

Aqua composed herself as best she could, wiped the tears from her eyes, rose from her chair with her body held taut and straight, and walked out, taking care not to look at Arthur again as she did so.

Chapter 24
Delta Dissembles

Arthur looked at his watch. It was now a quarter to nine. He had to move quickly to see all the others before nightfall. Gilles came in to check, bringing him a cup of coffee.

'And 'ow is it going, Artour? Are you getting nearer to a solution?' Gilles was worried that Arthur might be taking on too much and wanted to help as much as possible, but he needed clear instructions.

'I just need to see Delta, Eleanor, Steve and Chris, preferably in that order. After that we can probably stop for the night, but I will have to continue tomorrow.'

Gilles left quickly and returned very shortly afterwards with Delta. She had maintained her poise and sat down, perched on the end of the chair, bird-like, as if to bounce off and flutter into the air at any moment. She stared at Arthur, somewhat aggressively.

'I understand you want to see me, but I cannot understand why.'

'I just have to ask you a few routine questions, Delta. I recall you were out in the garden when Rock's body was found.'

'Yes, I was walking about with Steve, and we heard Maggie's screams, so we came over as soon as possible. I don't think there's anything unusual about that.'

'No, there isn't, Delta. But, can I ask, was there anything unusual that you noticed before Rock was found? Did you see him? Was he on his own or with someone else? How did he appear to you?'

'No, I can't say I did. But Rock was always a funny old cove. Kept himself to himself, we never had any idea what he was thinking.'

'But you must have known about the gold he had discovered?'

Delta sat up bolt upright, her elegant neck stretched even further than usual.

'I haven't the slightest idea what you are talking about. I know nothing about Rock and any gold.'

'We do not have much time this evening, Delta. But my enquiries to date have made things pretty clear to me. Rock had discovered gold to the east of the Watermeadow Estate. Full stop. Are you telling me that you knew nothing about this whatsoever?'

'Well, it is true there was some gossip about gold being discovered. But that has been around for well over a hundred years. I can't say I took much notice about it. I had other things on my mind.'

'These other things on you mind – did they involve Steve in any way?'

Delta flushed. This questioning was making her annoyed. She shook her head, and her long chestnut hair flared.

'I have no idea what you are talking about. Who you gossip with in this house is up to you. Whether you believe them is another matter. Steve and I are friends. What is wrong with that?'

'Nothing, of course. But just to clarify, you were with Steve when you heard Maggie scream, or had you gone your own way by then?'

'No, I was with Steve.'

'And where exactly where you in the estate when you heard Maggie?'

Delta flushed again.

'I really have no idea. I do not carry a map with me when I walk in the grounds. Why are you so interested in this? Does it have any relevance whatsoever in Rock's death?'

'Thank you for answering my questions, Delta. That will be all for the time being, but I want you to remember carefully the events of today, as I would like to see you again tomorrow.'

Delta tried to find an appropriate repartee, but failed. So she stormed out instead.

Chapter 25
Eleanor Hides Behind Rules

Eleanor came into Arthur's room, escorted by Gilles. She was at her most furious; everything had turned out so badly on her most precious day, and here was this pettifogging detective playing games with people.

Arthur looked up. He could tell this was not going to be easy. He had more than his fill of angry solicitors in his daily work and would have to be careful.

'Thank you for coming in to see me, Eleanor. I know this must be very difficult for you but I do have to ask you a few questions this evening.'

'Be that as it may, but I cannot understand why they cannot wait until the morning. You in the police seem to have no regard for other's feelings. What possible reason can you have for putting us through this agony now, after such an awful day?'

'We are wasting time, Eleanor. I only need to establish your relationship with Rock and how much you knew about the gold on the Watermeadow Estate.'

Eleanor seethed; her body was trembling, so when Arthur looked at her, she looked ever so slightly blurred.

'Why should you want to know these? What possible relevance have they to the death of poor Rock?'

'They could have every possible connection. We know – already – that you were seeing a lot of Rock in recent weeks and that you must have discussed his excavations in the estate. Were these discussions over the discovery of gold?'

'I am not at liberty to discuss confidential information shared with my clients. This is quite out of order.'

Arthur was getting exasperated. The ability of the legal profession to avoid simple answers to simple questions never ceased to amaze him.

'I will put it more directly, Eleanor. Did you know about the gold that Rock had discovered?'

'You are asking two questions, Arthur, not one. Did I know about something about gold and, if knowledge about this metal did exist, did I know that Rock had been responsible for its identification and discovery? I do wish you detectives did not get so confused.'

Arthur was trying hard not to lose his temper. There was no good reason for this procrastination.

'To save time, Eleanor, I am going to presume you know the answers to these questions and that they are both positive. Your discussions with Rock were related to the legal position of the gold on the Watermeadow Estate and also what proportion of the gold, if it was sold, would be attributed to the Watermeadow Estate.'

'I haven't the slightest idea what you are talking about,' said Eleanor snuffily.

'You know perfectly well what I am talking about, Eleanor. And was it you who decided that 40% of the proceeds of the gold would go to Rock; a very high proportion if I may say so?'

'I have no idea where you got this confidential information from. It is an absolute scandal that you have been eavesdropping on private conversations with my client.'

Now Arthur was furious too.

'Your client is dead, Eleanor. I am trying to find the reason why. You are obstructing justice by avoiding questions that are in your province to answer, and would have to answer if you were in court. You and I both know your answers are evasive and that you are not helping the cause of justice by acting in this way. I am not going to continue my questions now but will insist on seeing you tomorrow. Could you reflect on what you have said, and more particularly, have not said, and we will continue this conversation in the morning.'

Eleanor rose to her feet, stony-faced. But as she went out of the room, she had the feeling she had won.

Arthur was weary, and now preoccupied by doubt. He really did wonder if he had taken on too much on his own. If he could not solve the mystery of Rock's death quickly, he would miss the third test between England and Australia next Thursday at Old Trafford, and the chance to see Bradman in his last season. He had organised this leave well in advance and now there was a danger he would be tied up next week in something he could have avoided – if he not dived in at Watermeadow. But he must drive on. There were two more possible suspects he had to interview before the end of the evening while they had no possibility of communicating.

Chapter 26
Steve Is Just the Under-Gardener

Gilles came in with Steve. He was one of the staff at the Watermeadow Estate that Gilles could never work out properly. He just seemed to melt into the landscape, always around but never prominent, and without seeming to have opinions or views. He was even more mysterious than Rock.

He came in, still wearing his cap, nodding his head in apparent supplication before he sat down. Arthur was pleased. At least he would be less liked barbed wire than Eleanor.

'How long have you been working at Watermeadow, Steve?'

'Eight years now.'

'So you have a good idea what is going on in the estate?'

'Not really, I just help out in the garden.'

'But you have your nose to the ground, Steve, in more ways than one, so you must pick up on things.'

'Not sure what you're getting at.'

'Let's get down to the basics, Steve. You must have known about the gold.'

'What gold?'

Arthur was now getting irritable again.

'Everyone seems to know about the gold, Steve. It's an open secret. I am sure you would have known as well.'

'No. I can't say I did. I'm just the under-gardener.'

'I ask you again. Did you have any idea that there was the possibility of gold being found on the Watermeadow Estate?'

'I think I may have heard about the possibility of gold, as you put it. But as I am the under-gardener, I don't take much notice.'

Arthur realised this line of questioning was going nowhere. The under-gardener was going to remain under wraps.

'All right, I will leave this for the time being. Can I just ask you another question? How well do you know Lady Delta?'

'Hardly at all, really. I know her as a member of the family.'

'It is a strange world, isn't it, Steve? When people live in large families, they can sometimes get very close to one another. I have heard from others that you have been spending quite a lot of time with Lady Delta. Can I ask, are you close?'

Steve automatically touched his cap in supplication.

'Not sure what you mean by that. If you mean, were we friends, yes, we were. Lady Delta doesn't meet many people of her own age and gets a bit lonely. But I can't see what that has to do with Rock.'

'I seem to recall you were out with Delta in the garden when Rock's body was discovered, so this may have something to do with Rock.'

'I don't know what you are talking about. I am just an under-gardener, and my job is to do what needs to be done in the garden. I feel better in the garden than in the house, and Delta often feels the same. So it's not surprising we were in the garden at the time.'

Arthur looked at his watch. He had no more time with another evasive witness.

'That is all for the time being, Steve. I would like to see you in the morning again.'

'Then, can I please go back to my cottage in the grounds? I've never been in this house overnight. It's all very strange to me.'

Arthur got up quickly, went to the door and called Maggie in.

'No, I'm sorry, Steve. Everybody has to stay here tonight as we have to regard the gardens as a crime scene that must not be disturbed. Maggie, can you arrange for Steve to stay here tonight? I am sure you have enough bedrooms.'

'No problem at all, Arthur.' She turned to Steve. 'We'll put you up in the turret bedroom, you get a marvellous view of the garden from there.'

Steve and Maggie left, Steve disgruntled but Maggie excited again at the words Arthur had just spoken – "crime scene".

Chapter 27
Chris Gives a Glimpse of His Vision

It was now after 9.30pm. The last remnants of daylight were slowly dissipating outside the window as Arthur was about to interview his last witness, Chris (Capability) Challis. Chris entered, puffing his chest out to demonstrate a modicum of self-importance, but he only succeeded in resembling an overgrown turkey.

'It is good to see you, Chris. I am sorry you have had such a long time waiting, but I do not think I need keep you long.

'First of all, just to get things clear in my mind, you are often known as Chris Capability here, aren't you? Why is that?'

Chris was pleased he had addressed his favourite subject.

'It's just an honour that some people have picked up. I have always been fascinated by Capability Brown and his magnificent gardens. I know they have gone out of fashion recently, but anyone who has been to those magnificent gardens, such as those in Chatsworth or Brocklesby Park, must realise that their planning was a work of genius. So I have tried to do the same with Watermeadow. Of course, I will never come up to the standard of Capability Brown, but it is nice that some people think of me in the same sort of way.

Capability is my hero, my guide, my reason for being here...'

Arthur felt he had to interrupt.

'Quite, quite, Chris. But you are over-modest. These are very impressive gardens. You must know every inch of them by now. But can I ask you about Rock? You have both been working at Watermeadow for a long time now. How did you get on with him?'

'We each had our jobs to do. He looked after the soils and the drainage issues, and I looked after the trees and all the planning. It was just a working relationship.'

'Yes, but were you aware of his prospecting for gold in the grounds?'

'I'm not sure why you bring that up. What's that got to do with Rock?'

Arthur sighed.

'Chris, I want you to be honest with me. Everybody I have seen this evening has admitted they knew about Rock looking for gold in the estate. For some reason they were not always very forthcoming about this, so could I ask you directly, did you know that Rock had found gold somewhere in, or around the vicinity of, the Watermeadow Estate?'

Chris hesitated before responding.

'Yes, I think we all knew, in one form or another, but it was never discussed openly. We knew that Rock had been asked by Lord Watermeadow to investigate whether there was any gold around, but we did not really think that he would be successful. After all, I know these gardens like the back of my hand but have never seen any hint of any type of soil that might have gold deposits, so I felt that it was all going to go nowhere.'

'But it looks as though you were wrong. I understand from Lord Watermeadow that he was going to announce the discovery of gold this afternoon, had it not been for Rock's unfortunate death.'

'I didn't know about that. But I had some idea that this might be the case as everyone seemed so exciting about something and gold was the obvious subject.'

'So, if gold was discovered here on the estate, would its extraction be a problem for you?'

'Not if it was well away from the estate and was underground. That's where all the work has been to date, so far as I know.'

'And Rock had never discussed with you how he wanted to mine the gold?'

'No, absolutely not. He wouldn't have consulted me anyway. All his connections were with Lord Watermeadow. Once he knew, I would be informed.'

'Did that seem appropriate to you? After all, you are in charge of the estate.'

Chris was getting restless.

'No, I am employed to look after the estate, but that is all. Matters that concern the estate are relayed to me by Lord Watermeadow, nobody else. But I know, in my bones, that the estate is my creation, and I am its true custodian.'

'Thank you, Chris. I am glad to say that is all for this evening.'

Chris got up, somewhat excited and distracted, and left the room to be greeted by Maggie, who diligently showed him to his temporary bedroom. She returned to find Gilles talking to Arthur intently. They looked up as she entered.

'Ah, Maggie, I think you should join us,' said Arthur, not exactly conspiratorially, but that is how Maggie read it.

'I am far from sure what is going on here, but I think it is essential that Frothy, Aqua, Delta, Eleanor, Steve and Chris are all confined to the house overnight, so I hope you can lock all the doors. I also would like some information about the estate. How many buildings are there away from Watermeadow House?'

Maggie couldn't wait to respond.

'Well, there's the annexe where Chris and Steve live, but that's right next to the house. Then all the other buildings are really temporary. There's the summerhouse put up by Chris near the Mound so people can have a good view of the estate, and there's a hut over to the east where Rock used to keep his specimens. Nothing much else, I don't think.'

'Could you and Gilles go around the estate now and visit these places? You may need a torch as its getting dark now, but I want you to bring anything you see that is out of the ordinary back to me. And, before I forget it, can you also check the dustbins I saw outside to see if anything unusual is in them?'

Gilles and Maggie were only too pleased to help.

'Do not worry, mon ami. We 'ave an idea what you are looking for. And we will make sure nobody escapes. We cannot 'ave, how you say, people interfering with ze evidence.'

Within a minute, Gilles and Maggie had their coats on and were working out their coordinated routes around the estate. Arthur at last had two amateur sleuths he could rely on.

He could retire to bed in the knowledge he was not working entirely on his own. That was a very comforting thought that would allow him to sleep well after a remarkable day.

Chapter 28
Frothy Gets Wrong-Footed

The morning of 4th July was bright but fairly cool, and this allowed the opportunity for all to be energetic. Maggie and Gilles had carried out their tasks well and had found several items that Arthur judged to be of interest, for reasons that he would not fully explain. They had assembled all the guests for breakfast, and as they sat making desultory conversation, it was clear each was more preoccupied with their own thoughts than the conversation of others.

It was soon time to start the interviews again.

Frothy guessed he would be first on the list and was feeling increasingly uncomfortable about it. Maggie seemed to have taken on the mantle of Arthur's aide-de-camps and was watching everybody carefully at breakfast and even, most unprofessionally, listening into conversations. Frothy had been unable to talk to Aqua about the interviews yesterday evening, and it was clear she was quite upset this morning. For a man who liked to appear to be in charge, even if it was transparently obvious he was not for most of the time, this situation was not at all to his liking.

At times like this he wanted to escape. His mind always flipped back to the time he was at public school. He was not a popular boy, and it did not help matters that he could not control his emotions. When he was upset, he cried – he could not stop himself – and it did not take long for him to be rechristened Lord Waterbaby. He tried to make up for it by being a tough guy on the rugby field, but this did not help much as tears even flowed after he had suffered under crunching tackles when in full pursuit of the goal line. The only consolation was the communal bath after each match. When there, he could disappear under water for minutes on end – he always had good respiratory reserve – and cut himself off, paddling free in a silent wilderness, free from the troubles of ordinary life.

So he imagined himself protected in the warm dirty water of the bath as he was beckoned into the interview room by Arthur.

'There are just two matters I want to explore with you, this morning, Frothy. The first concerns the purchase of the Hawton Six. I understand that Rock had found gold fairly close to the Watermeadow boundary. So, assuming you just wanted to make sure you wanted the gold to be found on your property, a subject I am not going to follow up today, why did you need to buy all six acres?'

Frothy had to come up from his underwater utopia.

'It was all quite simple really. The lot at the auction was for six acres, so I made an offer for those.'

'But you did not have to buy all of them. All that extra land that you did not really need.'

'Rock said to me that we would need the extra land as he was sure more gold would be found there, and so I assumed this was correct. I had no means of confirming if he was right or not.'

'Good, so Rock had a say in this. The second issue also concerns Rock. You told me yesterday that you and Rock had agreed that the proceeds of the gold would be split 60:40 in your favour. Was this insisted upon by Rock?'

'Well, difficult to say how it came about, but Rock felt quite strongly that 40% was the correct figure.'

'Was this a formal agreement? Was it put down in writing?'

'Yes. Rock had discussions with Eleanor about it, and a legal document was prepared, which we both signed.'

'Good, I would like to see that in due course. Were there any other provisions made, or extra clauses made as part of that agreement?'

Frothy wished he could go under water again.

'I'm not sure what you mean? It was a standard legal document.'

'But as you know, Frothy, all these documents are full of 'ifs'. I would like to know if there were any 'ifs' in the document that might apply to the agreement between you and Rock?'

'Not that I can recall.'

'I will be more direct, Frothy. Were there any clauses in the agreement that might alter the percentages between you and Rock?'

Frothy was alarmed – and angry.

'I know now what you are getting at, Arthur. You are suggesting that I bumped off Rock so I could get my hands on his gold. I think that is a quite disgraceful suggestion and you ought to be ashamed of yourself.'

'That was not the question asked, Frothy, but you have given me a useful answer. I will not be asking any more questions at this point, but I should be grateful if you now go with Gilles and find this written agreement you had with Rock.'

'Why should I go with Gilles? I am quite capable of getting this myself.'

'If you reflect on this, Frothy, you will realise why I am asking Gilles to go with you. He is helping me to collect evidence and I need him to have the original.'

Arthur came out with Frothy to see Gilles waiting.

'Gilles, there is an important document that Frothy is going to be giving you. It is an agreement that accounts for the distribution of the resources from mining activities at Watermeadow. Remember, I want the original, not a copy.'

Gilles nodded and left with Frothy following in high dudgeon and muttering about disloyalty.

Chapter 29
Aqua Is Aerated

As Aqua came into Arthur's interview room, she looked up and noticed a crack in the corner of the ceiling. She reminded herself that she must get in touch with her lovable and eccentric Italian builder, Margherita. She was the only female heritage builder in the East Midlands, but Aqua always chose her for work at Watermeadow as she had such style.

But what was she doing looking up at the ceiling? When she was nervous, she was always more distracted, and there was Arthur looking at her intently.

'I am not expecting to keep you very long this morning, Aqua, but I would like to follow up on some questions I asked you last night. You knew something about the gold and the arrangement that Frothy had made with Rock?'

'As I said yesterday, I knew about gold, but had no idea how much there was and how much it was worth. Frothy had also mentioned that Rock was asking, if not insisting, on a share for discovering it.'

'Have you any idea how much the share being discussed was?'

'Well, the first time it was discussed, Frothy said it was about a half.'

'And what did you think of that?'

Aqua became animated.

'I thought it was absolutely ridiculous and made my feelings very clear. After all, Rock was asked to look for the gold by Frothy, so it was hardly fair to say he was the sole discoverer. What really annoyed me was the way in which

Rock was able to manipulate Frothy in all sorts of ways and get exactly what he wanted.'

'So would it be fair to say that you thought Rock was untrustworthy and grasping?'

'Yes, absolutely, grasping is the word. He seemed to resent everybody else at Watermeadow, was always complaining to the staff about being underpaid and stirring up trouble for us, and so once he had the upper hand in anything, we knew it would become very difficult for us.'

Arthur needed to encourage her further.

'But he should not have had the upper hand. He was only an employee.'

'Absolutely, but you would not have guessed it from the way he spoke to Frothy. The trouble is that Frothy is the worst negotiator in the world. He's lovable, but soft, and he always sees the other person's point of view rather than his own. And when he is put under pressure, he always caves in. So I know that he would always come out worst in any discussions with Rock, especially when he was being advised by Eleanor.'

'But Eleanor is only the family solicitor. She is employed by you, not by Rock.'

Aqua laughed sardonically.

'Yes, but you would hardly think so. For the past few months, she's been in and out, having discussions with Rock and to some extent with Frothy too. But Frothy and I have both felt she has been negotiating with us on behalf of Rock, not the other way round. At times I have been left fulminating, and I mean fulminating, by their behaviour.'

Aqua was now breathing heavily and feared she was flushing.

'All that is very illuminating, Aqua. But I cannot let this subject go without asking you this question. Is it not better for you and Frothy for Rock to be out of the way?'

Aqua burst into tears, despite trying not to.

'I knew you would have to mention this. You can be very cruel indeed, Arthur. But the fact that I didn't like Rock, and never pretended to like him, does not mean I wanted him dead. A death, particularly a murder, at Watermeadow, is a scandal that will be a stain on the family for years, no matter what you find in the course of your investigations, which I have to add are becoming increasingly tiresome.'

'You mentioned the word "murder", Aqua. Nobody knows whether Rock died from natural causes or was murdered. Why do you say "murder"?'

Aqua now exploded into rage, something to which she was very prone, which was one of the reasons why Frothy tried to accommodate her concerns in their daily living.

'You are now being preposterous. I say "murder", Arthur, because everyone in this house is now talking about murder. We have no idea if Rock was murdered or not, but everybody suspects this, so it is bound to be a subject we discuss. And it will go on being a subject we talk about until you, or somebody else, sorts it out. I must say, Arthur, you have made virtually no progress in your investigations so far, and I am very disappointed in you. I personally think you should hand this over to other colleagues in the police department as you are manifestly failing in your enquiries.'

'Thank you for your views, Aqua. I have noted them but can assure you that progress is being made. You have been part of this progress, despite your protestations, so I can finish this interview now.'

Aqua really wanted to continue sparring. But clearly, she could not. She rose from the chair, turned very smartly, and walked out with her nose, very so slightly, in the air.

Chapter 30
Delta Comes Clean

It was time to interview Delta again.

She entered, confidently, with the same mixture of scorn and aggression that she had shown before. Arthur realised he was going to have to be firm.

Arthur: 'I have made some progress in my investigation, Delta, and need you to be quite honest in your answers to my questions.'

Delta (primly): 'I always am honest.'

'There are no other members of the family present, and I am not going to go around telling tales. But from what I have heard already from others, I know that you have been seeing more of Steve Pitchfork than I would suspect if you were just casual friends. I have no wish to pry, but I need you to clarify one or two matters.'

'I said we are just friends.'

'I have seen you looking at him, Delta. You are not just friends. I put it to you that you are (pausing for effect) lovers.'

Delta looked at him angrily, then paused and took a deep breath.

'Well, what if we are? The trouble with this stuck-up family, with snobbery dripping out of every pore, is that I can't admit my feelings about him to anyone. I'd be thrown out – literally!'

'And, of course, you would have no way of supporting yourself. So if you were able to lay your hands on some, what shall I say, additional assets, things would be very different?'

'I don't know what you mean,' said Delta, knowing exactly what he meant.

'We have already discussed the matter of gold. It is still not at all clear to me who knew about the gold, where it happens to be and how much it is worth. But if someone knew where it was, and Rock was no longer around, the possibility of cashing in, if I can use such a vulgar term, would be very strong.'

Delta leant forward and looked Arthur straight in the eye.

'Are you suggesting, Arthur Mansfield, brilliant detective that you are, that I have planned to kill Rock Solid in order to get hold of his gold?'

'I am not alleging anything of the sort. All I am doing is putting forward hypotheses. This is one of them. There are dozens of others, all equally plausible. The reason I am putting this to you now is so that you can exclude this particular hypothesis, or, if you wish, support it in some way.'

'All right, I will give you some answers. If I am in love with Steve, and at this point I am neither denying nor admitting it, then I admit it would help if we had some more money. But what has that to do with the gold? It's all a mystery, as you have admitted. We do not seem to know anything about it, and all your allegations are going nowhere, because there is nothing to back them up. All the family know that if there is a great deal of gold or treasure hidden away somewhere, then we would all get the benefit of it. There would be no need to get rid of Rock or anyone else.'

'I fully agree with you, Delta. But I could not help noticing that you mentioned the word "treasure" as well as gold. What makes you think there is some sort of treasure as well?'

Delta scoffed.

'Gold and treasure are all part of the same. You really are getting very picky in your choice of words, Mr Mansfield.'

'I don't think I am, Delta. There are some important differences between "treasure" and "gold", but at this point, I would just say it was a slip of the tongue on your part. I think that will be all for the time being.'

Delta made as if to say more, but thought better of it, and left hurriedly.

Chapter 31
Eleanor Is Exposed

Arthur was getting frustrated. His interviews were going well in one way, but he was getting no nearer to a solution, and he could see everybody was getting restive. He would continue his efforts but might have to give up shortly and hand over the problem to his colleagues. But why was he thinking like this? A murder was a murder, and they were getting fewer in number, so he must reactivate his detective's brain, get those investigative neurons ticking again, and link all the facts together. Sherlock Holmes was a fiction, but he was a great detective – because he looked for evidence and listened carefully. When he thought about it, he was convinced he had all the evidence here in Watermeadow. He might have to cut a few corners, but he was sure the culprit was one of those he had already interviewed.

The next was Eleanor, and with her he hoped for a breakthrough. She came in with her usual haughty expression, looking down at him in a lopsided way as though he was an alien being, before she sat down.

'Good morning, Eleanor. I hope I will not detain you long.'

'I should think not,' said Eleanor tartly. 'I have to tell you that I, and the other members of the family, are simply fed up with your investigation, if it can be deemed as such as it is so chaotic. By detaining us here against our will, you are denying us *habeas corpus,* and I am afraid action will be taken against you accordingly if you do not release us.'

'I quite understand your frustration, Eleanor. Believe me, it is getting to me too. But perhaps you can hurry things on a little by explaining what you mean by this letter that you have recently received.'

Arthur unfolded a small crumpled sheet of paper and smoothed it out on the table in front of Eleanor.

'This is a letter dated 17th June, 1948.

Dear Eleanor,

Thanks for your latest letter. I did not realise that we had any substantial family heirlooms, but I am quite happy to help out with your request. I think the best arrangement...'

'Just a moment, Arthur. You have purloined a personal letter of mine. Hand it back immediately or I shall call the police.'

'Please bear with me, Eleanor, and just in case you have forgotten, I am a representative of the police. This letter was not in your possession. It was found in one of the bins outside Watermeadow House yesterday. May I continue?'

Eleanor was too consternated to reply and settled back in the chair in uncharacteristic confusion.

'I think the best arrangement is for you to pack the goods personally and send them to me by special delivery to the Consulate here in Geneva. If you attach a prominent label "for the personal attention of Edwin Montagu", it will ensure that...'

'This is where the page ends. The rest of the letter seems to have disappeared. Would you like to give me some more information about "the goods" mentioned in this letter? Would you like to describe to me exactly what they are?'

'I most certainly would not. It is none of your business. I will not have you intruding into a personal and private matter.'

'I think it would be in your interests to be a little more forthcoming, Eleanor. If there is an innocent explanation for this letter, we can move on. If there is not, I can only assume that it is bound up in some way with Rock's death. So I ask you again, can you give a fuller explanation of the goods you were planning on sending to (he checked the letter again)

Edwin, whom I presume is a member of the extended Montagu family?'

'Yes, Edwin is my brother. But I would be breaking family confidences if I told you about the family heirlooms. They are very precious and highly personal.'

'Precious and personal to some, but equally precious to many others, I suppose. But as you have chosen not to tell me anything more, I cannot press you. But think about this very carefully, Eleanor. Hiding evidence in connection with a crime is itself a crime.'

Eleanor had had enough.

'I have just had enough of your threats and insinuations, Arthur Mansfield. Unless you allow us all to go immediately, I am going to ask that you be prosecuted for unlawful detention. I live in a democracy, not a Communist country, where the rule of law means nothing, and I mean to exercise my rights.'

'I will finish my enquiries very shortly. Please let me accompany you to the door as I would like to say something to all the people here at Watermeadow House.'

Arthur shepherded Eleanor to the door, a process made more difficult by Eleanor swatting his arm and striding forcefully into the hall. She was not a person who would allow herself to be patronised by anybody.

Arthur raised his voice so that all could hear.

'I do apologise for the delay. I have almost finished by interviews and would like everybody to assemble in the large drawing room at 12 noon, when I hope to conclude my investigation and allow you all to go. Please be patient; I do not want to make any mistakes over such an important matter.'

There were a few grumbling noises but no obvious dissent. But Arthur realised he was running out of time and inspiration had to come to him soon if he was to solve what was becoming a very mysterious crime.

Chapter 32
Steve Has an Interesting Explanation

Steve Pitchfork came in, looking furtive and still wearing his cap, even though this was now quite unnecessary.

Arthur needed to get a move on.

'During my enquiries I have found out a great deal, Steve, and one thing I have learned is that you probably know more about the goings-on in and around the Watermeadow Estate than almost anybody else here.'

'Nice of you to say so, Mr Mansfield,' said Steve, reflexly touching his cap.

'So you must have known quite a bit about Rock's prospecting for gold.'

'Not as much as you might think. Remember, Mr Mansfield, I'm just the under-gardener and my job is…'

'Yes, I know, Steve, "to look after the gardens", but you must have noticed where he was going and what he was doing. After all, he spent most of his time in the garden, or under it, if I could put it that way, and even you must have been curious.'

'I suppose I saw what was going on. But it didn't make much of an impression on me. As long as he wasn't interfering in my job and I wasn't interfering in his, we just continued on our usual ways.'

'I am going to move you on this matter a little further, Steve. I have just received this piece of paper – it was found in your hut the other day after I asked Gilles to collect information – but it does not make much sense to me.'

Steve looked bemused, but he was also on edge, and Arthur noticed his hands were trembling slightly. He was being taken outside his standard comfort zone of just being the under-gardener.

Arthur produced a piece of squared paper with just a few symbols on it. This is what was shown:

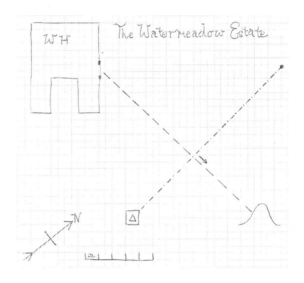

'Now, can you explain what this means, Steve? It really doesn't make sense to me, but I presume the letters on the left indicate Watermeadow House?'

'Can I look at that again, Mr Mansfield?' Steve leant forward, turned the paper round, looked at it quizzically for a few seconds, and the explanation suddenly came to him.

'This is just a rough map of the Watermeadow Estate. Yes, you are right. Watermeadow House is on the left of the drawing. It's all related to a tree order. Chris ordered three Japanese hornbeams, as he liked the foliage, and these are the positions on the estate I chose for them.'

'But this drawing does not indicate where the trees should go.'

'Well, you've already said, Mr Mansfield, I know the Watermeadow Estate very well, so I don't need any landmarks. That was all I needed to know exactly where to plant them.'

'But I thought from my conversations with Chris that when it came to placing new trees in the estate, he was the person who was in charge. You know, it had to fit in with the ambience of the gardens. He was very fussy about that.'

'Yes, but as these were just three Japanese hornbeams, he left the decision to me.'

'So this had nothing to do with Rock and his plans to look for gold on the Watermeadow Estate?'

'No, Rock had nothing to do with this. He did not have any part in the planning of the gardens. He just told us where he would like to make his tunnels, and Chris and I chose the places which created the least interference.'

'Thank you, Steve, as time is running short, I will stop there. I only have one more interview and so will see you again shortly.'

'Thank you, Mr Mansfield,' said Steve, touching his cap again as he rose from the chair. 'And can I say, I wish you all the best in your investigation.'

'Thank you, Steve,' said Arthur with genuine warmth. 'It is not an easy task being a detective, and we get more brickbats than praise, but it is good to get encouragement from time to time.'

Chapter 33
Chris Goes Past the Point

It was now half-past eleven. Arthur had one more interview before he saw all the possible suspects at 12 noon. But first, he had another task for his assistant, Gilles. He called him in.

'Gilles, I hope you can help me, but you have to be very quick. Here is the map, or drawing, that you found in Steve's hut yesterday.'

'Yes, I know. It makes no sense, but you said, collect all the evidence, toutes les preuves, all the proof, so I kept it for you.'

'It may be important. Steve said it just marks the places where he planted three hornbeams on the estate. But I find this hard to believe. I think there must be another explanation. So could you take this out and look around, and see if you can work out what it is? And if you find anything else in the huts, no matter what it is, please bring it back to me.'

'Yes, mon ami. I go immediately.' Gilles left swiftly; this was going to be a challenge.

Chris was sitting on his own, looking aimless. He had to be escorted into Arthur's room.

'My questions are going to be fairly short, this morning, Chris. First I would like to ask you about the different responsibilities you and Steve have on the Watermeadow Estate.'

'It is quite simple. My job is to oversee the estate and to make sure that everything remains, or becomes, exactly as Capability Brown would have liked it. Steve, as the under-gardener, just keeps the garden in order and does what I ask him to do.'

'So when you order new trees for the estate, do you decide where they ought to be planted?'

'Yes, absolutely and definitely. If the symmetry of the gardens is changed in any way, it would be an abomination, and I do not use that word lightly.'

'So there would be no circumstances in which Steve would decide where to plant trees quite independently?'

'Absolutely not. If you have any evidence of that, I should like to know immediately.'

'Thank you, Chris. That is very helpful. Now can I return to the impact of Rock's work on the estate? What was your reading of the work that Rock was going to do?'

'I am the follower, or you could say, the disciple of Lancelot Brown, who, in his work 200 years ago, changed the face of the English country garden. Can I ask you, Arthur, do you have a garden?'

'Yes, I do, but it is fairly small and it is not really relevant…'

Chris interrupted.

'Of course, it is relevant. And, doubtless, you have a little lawn, and a flower border, and a separate plot for the vegetables if you are so inclined.'

'Yes, but…'

'No, this is not the time for a "but". Lancelot Brown showed us how to make a garden real, to infiltrate it into our very beings, to make it part of our souls, to bring us into complete harmony with our environment. Not for him the little lawn with its fancy edgings, not for him the bedding plants equally spaced in the borders like soldiers on parade, but instead the sweeping vistas, the glorious panoramas, the feel of the grass and woodlands and water at your feet, that none of your little gardens can ever hope to achieve.'

'I am not arguing with you about this, Chris, but I would like to ask you a few more questions, only a few. Were you concerned that all the talk about, and work associated, with the gold might affect the Watermeadow Estate?'

'No, nothing can ever really change the Watermeadow Estate. It has been brought from the wild into civilisation and now it has the Capability Brown stamp, it has become indelible. You may think this is illusory, and I know that there are always looters hiding in the shadows waiting to destroy, but once we have the Lancelot Brown image, it will survive, indefinitely.'

'You are not quite answering my question, Chris'.

'Why should I answer your footling questions when there is something much bigger all around us? The people who spend almost all the time in this little house do not have the feel of the gardens all around, a vast envelope of interweaving patterns that raise our souls above the other animals and bring us into the uplands of understanding.'

Arthur now fully realised that this interview was going absolutely nowhere, and, in any case, it was nearly 12 noon.

He needed to see Gilles first. He hoped that he had found something useful on his second round of travels; the solution to Rock's murder was as far away as ever.

Chapter 34
Arthur Sets Out the Stall

It was 12 o'clock. The bells of Hawton Church rang the midday hour after the Sunday service, not quite in tune, but they were over four hundred years old.

Maggie and Emmy had ushered all into the drawing room, where they sat, roughly in what could be called social order, with Frothy and Aqua in the front, Delta and Eleanor behind, and Steve and Chris at the rear by the door. But Chris seemed very distracted and restless, and kept rising from his chair, going out and coming back in again.

Arthur was getting nearer to the answers, and he was pleased that he had persisted in his investigation and not just handed it over to the rest of the constabulary to deal with. They would have taken an age to complete and incurred great cost. At a time of national indigence, any savings were highly desirable. But he must not get over-confident or go beyond the evidence. If he did, he would miss the Test at Old Trafford and his last glimpse of Don Bradman.

He cleared his throat.

'I am seeing you all here today as you are still suspects in this investigation. As no doubt you have gathered since yesterday, the death of Rock Solid was not through natural causes. He was murdered. I will come to the exact cause of his death later.

'I am not sure at this point whether the murderer is single or plural, but I will outline the case against each of you. First of all, Frothy, you had an obvious motive. You were desperate to have as much money as possible from the sale of gold from the Watermeadow Estate, and the only person who really stood in your way was Rock. He had demanded a much larger percentage than you expected from the sale. I do not know why the percentage was so large, and I suspect Eleanor had something to do with it…'

Eleanor jumped up. 'That is a slanderous suggestion. Please withdraw it immediately.'

'Sit down, Eleanor, your time will come, but it is not now.'

'So if Rock was out of the way, by whatever means, the proceeds from the sale of the gold would come to the Watermeadow Estate. I have seen the formal agreement signed by Rock and you, Frothy, which makes this quite clear. The payment to Rock was for a proportion of his services rendered; if he was not around for its receipt, that could not be helped. It was a payment to Rock and Rock alone. So you had a clear motive for murder, Frothy, that cannot be denied.'

'I do deny it, Arthur.' Frothy's voice was croaking in distress, and all these revelations were being aired in front of the others. It was terrible. 'A motive for murder, in your language, may be regarded as an intention to kill, but that could not be further from reality.'

'I agree with you, Frothy. A motive is not enough. But I have to put the case against you, as with each of you. In your case, Aqua, you felt that Rock was getting away with far too much of what you considered to be your money and did not feel that Frothy on his own was able to stand up to Rock's demands. So you could, either alone or in concert with Frothy, have organised his demise.'

Aqua was crying again. 'It is all quite preposterous,' she said through her tears. 'You have no understanding of how much you wound.'

'I am just putting the case forward, Aqua, not concluding it. When it comes to Delta, things become a little more difficult.

'This is because of her relationship with Steve. I am not going to disclose what I know about this relationship, as, being a discreet sort of fellow, I do not want to pry too deeply into personal matters when they are not my prime concern.'

'Well, you are certainly doing a good job of contradicting your own intentions,' said Delta tartly.

'No, I am protecting you, Delta. What I have to decide is whether your feelings for Steve were sufficient for you to enter into an arrangement whereby you combined forces, so to speak, to engineer Rock's death. You would only do this if you could be confident of laying your hands on the gold that seemed to be beckoning.'

'As for you, Eleanor, you are an intelligent woman and may have already suspected that I do not think you are being honest in maintaining that you are going to send your heirlooms to your brother in the diplomatic service in Geneva. Coincidences have to be explained, Eleanor, and in this instance, coincidence and cause are weakly separated.'

'You are talking in riddles, Arthur, as you frequently do, and I hope you end this nonsense of allegations very shortly.' Eleanor was not going to be cowed by anybody.

'As for Steve, he too might have had a motive, particularly if his relationship with Delta was blossoming to the extent that they might be thinking of, shall we say, branching out together. This, of course, would have financial implications, but I need not say any more at this juncture.'

Steve touched his cap again, as if to indicate that he was indeed the person under discussion.

'Finally, we come to Chris. I cannot be sure what is going on in Chris's mind, but what is clear is that he is very fond of the Watermeadow Estate and does not want it disturbed in any meaningful way. How much it would be disturbed by the gold ventures is very difficult to say, but it is certainly a matter of concern to him.

'So these are the reasons why I have asked you so many questions in the last 18 hours. I am now going to ask Maggie and Emmy to come in with some strong coffee, or tea if you prefer, and then I will move on to some more explanations.'

Chapter 35
Arthur Concludes with a Finale

Maggie and Emmy had duly brought in the coffee, and everyone was ready. Maggie asked if she was allowed to sit at the back of the room. 'Of course,' said Arthur, 'you have been a valuable assistant, as has Gilles, so bring him in too.'

'Good, with all assembled, we can clarify some important matters. The first is the obvious one, the gold. I do not think this exists in the grounds of Watermeadow or its surroundings.'

'This is complete nonsense, Arthur. Are you on the same planet?' expostulated Frothy, whose gout was now beginning to act up.

'Let us consider the evidence. Rock brought some tiny flakes of gold to you a few months ago. We do not know if he actually found the gold in the Watermeadow marshes or he just pretended he had. We can never know, but since that original discovery, who has actually seen any gold in the form that it normally occurs? No, nobody, unless Rock was salting it away somewhere without anybody knowing.

'But it all made sense to many of you to think there was indeed a golden seam over to the east of Watermeadow. Rock was able to get all the chemicals to extract gold from gold ore, and, with Eleanor's help, was able to draw up legal agreements for Frothy to sign, and Delta and Steve could indulge in idle fantasy, but only up to a point.'

'But what was all the fuss about then?' said Maggie, then realising she should not have spoken – she was only an observer.

'The fuss, Maggie, if we can indeed call it that, was over something of potentially much greater value. Delta unfortunately let slip the word "treasure" when I interviewed her, but anyone of you could have said it at some time. There is, or has been, something of considerable value, we think, over to the east of the Watermeadow Estate. I could not work out why Frothy was wanting to buy all the Hawton Six when the gold had been found so close to the boundary of the estate. I guessed what was of value must be quite a bit further away.'

'How do you know all this?' asked Aqua. 'You have not given us any evidence.'

'Quite right, Aqua. It is mainly supposition up to this point. But here we bring in my most diligent apprentice, Gilles.

'It was Gilles who found a curious drawing in Steve's hut.

'Here it is – you will not be able to see it at the back – it has a series of crosses and an arrow. Steve tells me it was where he should have planted Japanese hornbeams.'

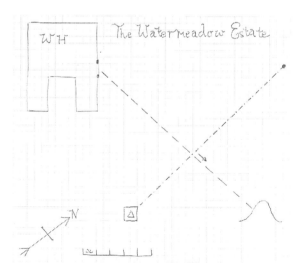

Chris woke up from his reverie at the back of the room. 'Nobody plants trees on the Watermeadow grounds without my permission. What is going on here? Who is despoiling, who is sabotaging us?'

'It might have been a different hornbeam, Chris,' said Steve, rather weakly in response.

Arthur continued. 'Now when Gilles investigated this map, or drawing, he could find no evidence of any new planting of hornbeams. And then he realised that the scale of the map was wrong. If you look just south of east from Watermeadow House, you can see the important distant landmark of Belvoir Castle, on the top of the hill to the right. When you have the distance of this in your mind, it is several miles, you can get the scale of the map from the squared paper. Gilles checked on the position of the lower Δ on the map and found it was the top of the Mound. By cross-checking the distances, a line from the Δ to the tallest tree in the South Willows wood was found to be at right angles to the line between Watermeadow House and Belvoir Castle. Once he had his bearings and could see Watermeadow House, the Mound and Belvoir Castle, he could work out exactly where the two lines crossed. So when he travelled a short distance to the east of this point, as the arrow suggested, he found something.'

'The treasure,' said Maggie inadvertently.

'Not exactly. Gilles noticed a lot of digging activity in the area that seemed to indicate that something had recently been buried there, in the middle of the meadow, but there was nothing there now.'

There was silence. Many of those seated looked at each other as observers in novels often say, "with meaning".

Arthur was looking carefully too.

'So, ladies and gentlemen, what has been going on here? Well, here we have a clue. He pulled out a booklet of what appeared to be pristine squared paper.

'Gilles brought this back to me this morning. It was found in Rock's hut. Gilles did not think it would be of interest, but it reveals a great deal. If you look at the top sheet, you will see it has a ragged edge showing that another sheet has been torn out above it. When you match the map drawing with the torn edge of the booklet, you see it is a perfect fit.'

'What are you on about, Arthur? This has nothing to do with the subject.' Frothy had lost all contact with what was going on and could only think of how awful the pain of gout was.

'It is central to the subject, Arthur. I put to you the obvious scenario. Rock has marked the position of the treasure – let us call it that for the moment – and leaves it in his hut, not thinking that anyone can decipher it. Steve, who is much cleverer than he makes out to be, tears the page out of the book and transfers it to his hut. Rock comes back later, notes that the map has gone but has no idea who has taken it. He decides the best thing to do is to go back, dig up the treasure, and hide it, or bury it, somewhere else. The last thing he wants is for someone else to make off with it.'

'You still have failed to give one scrap of evidence that this, whatever it is – if it exists, is valuable and can be called treasure,' said Aqua, who was now getting quite interested in Arthur's reasoning.

'No, you are right, Aqua. I am going to add one more supposition. I mentioned earlier that Eleanor is intending to send some valuable family heirlooms to her brother in Geneva. We were able to see a letter that her brother had written.'

'How do you know it was not a forgery?' said Eleanor.

'I will let that pass,' said Arthur. 'What is more important is the nature of these heirlooms. If Eleanor is able to show us exactly what she is sending to her brother, and why it is so special to the family, I will revise my view.

'To extend my supposition, my view is that Rock and Eleanor knew exactly what was in the so-called treasure, realised its potential value and conspired together to remove the valuable contents.'

'You are now in never-never land,' said Eleanor. 'Just one shaky theory after another, and then the whole lot will come tumbling down.'

'I have not finished yet, Eleanor. I put it to you that a strong case can be made for you having dug up the treasure to keep it for yourself, and completely without Rock's knowledge. They also serve who only dig and wait, and when everything had settled, you can make off for Geneva with a spring in your step.'

Eleanor was having none of this.

'Unless you withdraw that remark immediately, Arthur Mansfield, I will sue you for slander.'

'I only said a case could be made, Eleanor, not that a case had been made. But, if you wish, I will withdraw it.'

'But we have not discussed the possible contribution of Chris.

'I know he has been very concerned that the environment of Watermeadow should in no way be altered by the recent developments. He was particularly concerned about possible changes to the landscape after the discovery of gold.'

Chris was now animated again.

'Yes, mining just creates destruction – everywhere. That's what they've done in Australia. Just look at Kalgoorlie. You've probably never heard of it, but there they've just stripped the land and it totally bare. Not a thing is living, just a lot of greedy miners making a living while destroying the planet.'

'You have put the case eloquently, Chris. But I want to go further than this. I want to discuss how Rock died. I was lucky enough to be present just after his body was discovered, and I could not help noticing a smell of almonds.

'I thought this might be related to his death and now have the evidence. Again, I am indebted to my assistant, Gilles, who would be very welcome to join the Detective Constabulary at the Nottingham Police Department the next time we have a vacancy.'

Arthur produced a small bottle.

'Gilles found this on the floor of Chris's woodshed a short time ago. The label on it says "sodium cyanide". Sodium cyanide is used to treat gold ore, and I am sure that this was originally in Rock's hut. But it was found in Chris's hut.

Could it be that Chris had stolen the cyanide and put some of its crystals into Rock's champagne, knowing that it would combine with the acid in the champagne to make hydrocyanic acid, probably the most dangerous poison known to man, which can kill instantly? And, as you may know, it smells of almonds. Have you anything to say about this, Chris?'

Chris was now out of control. He rushed up to the front of the room and harangued Arthur.

'You, and all your friends, are the enemies of the environment. You pay lip service to it, pretending you are looking after it, but all the time are eating it away, with your policies about urban regeneration, new factories and new mines. Once you destroy the earth, it can never recover. So Rock was your agent, sent in to destroy Watermeadow, and now he has been destroyed.

'I have heard you, plotting away in your little corners, I've heard your voices, mocking me and Lancelot Brown, but we are fighting back. We are making a stand. I have to tell you, this is now war. We are no longer going to tolerate this wanton destruction, this pillaging of our plant-life, this depredation of all that we hold dear. So Rock is only the first of many to be sacrificed in this way.'

Before anyone could do anything, Chris pulled a bottle from his pocket. He waved it at the others.

'And do not think that I too can avoid sacrifice. I am with my mentor, my master, Lancelot Brown, the preserver of England's green and pleasant land, and I will join him in Capablia, the oasis of plenty in the skies, which will forever remain free from your despoliation.'

Chris took a deep drink from the bottle. Arthur and Frothy rushed over but it was too late.

'You cannot harm me now,' said Chris, smiling, before closing his eyes and never opening them again.

Chapter 36
Eleanor Avoids Obstruction

There was great shock, but also intense relief, among those at Watermeadow House. The ambulance had been called, the ambulance men had arrived, had taken the body of Chris away, but not after making an inappropriate joke about the free for all that might follow in the morning with the dawn of the new National Health Service. There was a subdued calm in the drawing room.

'I am very glad to say that you can now all leave,' said Arthur, smiling. 'I apologise for keeping you so long, and asking so many difficult questions, but you have been very patient with me. I hope you agree that your time has not been wasted. Sometimes a murder inquiry is best investigated immediately; I hope I have shown that to you. All of you are now free to leave, apart from Eleanor. I know I have put her through the mangle a little, but I just want to clear up one or two matters.'

Eleanor was now deflated. She was no longer the fighting cock taking on all comers. She had lost two irreplaceable prizes in the last two days, was she about to lose another?

She and Arthur went into the interview room again.

Arthur was now in a more kindly mood. The pressure was off him now that the murder had been solved, but Eleanor was still an important witness.

'I know you have been bothered by some of my questions, Eleanor, but hope you understand that I could not avoid asking them as you were a prime suspect in this investigation. What concerns me now is the remaining issue of the treasure, if I can still call it that. I think I am right in assuming that you know more than most about the exact nature of this treasure, and possible where it came from.

I am also concerned that your answers to date have not helped me, and there is a real danger that you could be charged with perverting the cause of justice. As a solicitor, you will know that fabricating or disposing of evidence, and conspiring with others with the intent of perverting the cause of justice, are serious offences. I would like to avoid a charge of this nature, as I know it would wreck your career, irrespective of the eventual outcome. So I would like you and I to have a frank discussion about the treasure and your original intentions. This conversation, if it successfully closes the inquiry, will remain completely confidential, and although you might expect me to say that, I do want to assure you, absolutely, that I would like nothing better to leave Watermeadow House in a short time with no further issues on my mind.'

Eleanor had lost the will to argue, but she was still very concerned about saying something that would incriminate her. After this appalling episode, she must still be able to hold her head up in the presence of her colleagues in the solicitor's office with no stain of any sort attached to her. And now there seemed to be little point in covering up her knowledge. It was all of no value to her now.

She took a deep breath.

'I will do my best to answer your questions – and I promise to be as accurate as possible in my replies.'

'Good,' said Arthur. 'I am not going to take any notes at this point but will let you know if I need to write anything down. Ideally, I want no record to be kept of this conversation.'

Arthur knew he was taking a risk in making this promise, but it was already very clear to him that Eleanor was a stickler in her pursuit of privacy, and by making these promises, he hoped she would be more forthcoming.

'First, could I ask you, have you seen what everybody has called "the treasure"?'

'No, I have not seen it,' said Eleanor clearly. 'But Rock has, sorry, I should say, had', she had a catch in her voice which showed the strain, 'seen it and told me what it contained.'

'Can you describe its contents, and the form in which it was left, more precisely?'

'I can only rely on Rock's verbal messages. He told me that the treasure was in an old sack, largely decomposed, but with an inscribed message "Treasure for King James" and something strange, probably in Latin, next to it. It contained some gold and silver coins, some candlesticks, also, he thought, in gold and silver, and some other silverware, mainly I think spoons and other cutlery.'

'And where did he find this treasure?'

'He found it in the place you have just been talking about, over in the meadow by the wood, about three quarters of a mile from Watermeadow House. It was the place where Gilles has just described.'

'And how did he come across the treasure?'

'He, as you know, was prospecting in the area and was taking soil samples. You do this in geology with a soil augur, which screws into the ground; you then pull it up and can see a core of soil at different levels. Rock was doing this in one place when he came across something much harder than he expected and when he pulled the augur up, here were some bits of sack attached to it. So he decided to dig more deeply in the area and exposed the sack with all its contents. He then realised how valuable it might be and buried it again as he thought this was the safest place for it to be.'

'As a solicitor, I am sure you fully understand what I am about to say. What Rock unearthed was indeed treasure, as coins and other objects in gold and silver over 300 years old are formally classified as such. What you also must know is that treasure as so defined is Crown property, not the finder's. I cannot remember the full details, but the finder may be entitled to a share of this, but only a minor one.'

'Yes,' said Eleanor softly, now very forlorn. 'I realised that too and, because of this, we decided not to tell anyone about it and pretend that we had continued to find gold to the east of the estate.'

'This is now getting to a sensitive point, Eleanor. Was it because of this knowledge you decided to see if you could send the contents of the sack, or at least some of them, to your brother in Geneva? It had crossed my mind that Switzerland was a very good place to dispose of antique jewellery.'

Eleanor breathed deeply again. This is where she had to be careful, but she also realised that Arthur would not take any more evasion.

'Yes. But I do not want this repeated anywhere. I was concerned that the treasure might be intercepted and felt that it should go through diplomatic channels – or at least look as though it was being sent that way. That was why I wrote the letter to Edwin. But I want to make it absolutely clear,' and here she looked imploringly at Arthur, 'that I did not send anything to Edwin and none of the jewellery or other goods ever came into my hands.'

'I am going to believe that, Eleanor, and, as such, that is not an offence. But where do you think the treasure is now?'

'I have absolutely no idea, and, to tell the truth, now I don't really care. You were right. Rock had noticed the map drawing had been removed and guessed it might be Steve or Chris who had taken it, so he immediately went out and reburied the treasure.'

'Have you any idea where?'

'No, and I don't want to know. Rock just said it was in a very safe place and as the other had been undetected for over 300 years, he was quite confident that the second place would be even safer.'

Arthur thought for a second or two.

'I have to say I am satisfied by your answers, Eleanor. I have no more questions, have made no notes of any sort, and I think you can regard this conversation as having taken place in the ether. No trace of it can ever be discovered. I think we are both agreed that knowledge of the treasure has not done anyone any good, and the sooner it can be expunged from all our minds, the better.'

Eleanor left the room with a weight lifted from her mind, and, oddly enough, from her body too. She was free of all this trouble at last and could start afresh again.

Arthur packed his bags, gave a special word of thanks to Gilles, Maggie and Emmy, who were still humming with excitement, made his farewells to Frothy and Aqua, and, with a sigh of anticipation, climbed into his Austin A40 and started the engine. Good, it had started first time. He had something to look forward to. At times it had seemed a long way off, but he would now definitely be able to see Don Bradman at Old Trafford.

Chapter 37
1879 – Hawton Church Is Closed
With a Message

In 1879 All Saints Church at Hawton was not an inviting place. The roof was leaking, the tower was unsafe, and the musty smell of decay pervaded the air as the congregation entered the church and took up their positions, rather diffidently, each side of the nave, every Sunday. They seated themselves in the same pews every week, mainly through habit, but also spread out a little, as though wanting the church to appear more populated than it actually was. And on this particular morning, Sunday, 13th April, Robert Washington, the rector, had some important news to deliver to the twelve stalwarts who were still regular communicants.

He took the service slowly, even more ponderously than his normal habit, for he wanted all his words to sink in. At the end of the service, he stood in front of the chancel with his arms half raised and waited for complete silence. Robert had a good sense of the dramatic, and this was an occasion for it to be put to use.

'I have a sombre message to deliver. The church is in such a state of disrepair that it will have to close temporarily for the safety of all. We are hoping for successful instigation of repairs but cannot be sure when these will be carried out, or, indeed, completed. So this will be the last service for a considerable time. Let us pray to God that it will be a short one, and we can soon meet again.'

As the congregation departed in some sorrow, Robert had to complete a number of tasks before locking the church. He had always been a pessimist and could not see how the church would reopen. The Diocese had no money, the parishioners were all of limited means and there was not a benefactor in sight. Some still talked about the Hawton treasure but it was all an illusion, conjured up by optimists who had nothing else to grab for their comfort.

He locked the north door and tidied the pews for the last time. But there was another task to carry out. He emptied the safe. Only a miserly shilling was there, together with a few documents. He was just about to close it when he saw what appeared to be an old rag pressed against the far end. He fished it out. It was a battered purse. He opened it and read,

'James lapides sacculi occultatum, inveniet faciem meam.'

He struggled to remember the Latin he now rarely used. 'James sack (or is it bag) hidden find me,' he muttered. 'Some sort of childish nonsense,' he said to himself, 'but how it got into the safe is a mystery.' He tossed it into the bin for disposal.

So despite all the suspicions, the mutterings, the sufferings, plottings and schemings, the expectations and anticipations, and the all-devouring frustrations and hopes of the people in Watermeadow House, the secret treasure of Hawton still remains undiscovered to this day. Rock was the only person who had seen the contents of the strange sack delivered in haste in 1603, and where it is now is an enigma. If Eleanor was to be believed, it is indeed a sack of gold and silver and other valuables gems from the prospective knights of Lincolnshire and Leicestershire. But we only have Rock's word, and it appears that he was never completely reliable. The answer is in the hands of its eventual discoverer. But whether its uncovering will bring joy at the same time is more difficult to guess. It did not seem to in 1948, so why should 2018, or indeed any other year, be different. Riches taunt and taint, and only briefly gratify.